GENERAL MURDERS

AMOS
WALKER
MYSTERIES

GENERAL MURDERS

Loren D. Estleman

HOUGHTON MIFFLIN COMPANY

BOSTON • 1988

For information about permission to reproduce selections from
this book, write to Permissions, Houghton Mifflin Company,
2 Park Street, Boston, Massachusetts 02108.

Library of Congress Cataloging-in-Publication Data

Estleman, Loren D.
General murders / by Loren D. Estleman.
p.   cm.
"Amos Walker mysteries."
ISBN 0–395–41071–1
1. Walker, Amos (Fictitious character) — Fiction.
2. Detective and mystery stories, American.   I. Title.
PS3555.S84G46 1988   88–1869
813'.54 — dc 19   CIP

Printed in the United States of America

P 10 9 8 7 6 5 4 3 2 1

To Bob Randisi

Contents

Greektown

THE RESTAURANT was damp and dim and showed every indication of having been hollowed out of a massive stump, with floorboards scoured as white as wood grubs and tall booths separated from the stools at the counter by an aisle just wide enough for skinny waitresses like you never see in Greektown. It was Greektown, and the only waitress in sight looked like a garage door in a uniform. She caught me checking out the booths and trundled my way, turning stools with her left hip as she came.

"You are Amos Walker?" She had a husky accent and large dark pretty eyes set in the rye dough of her face. I said I was and she told me Mr. Xanthes was delayed and sat me down in a booth halfway between the door and the narrow hallway leading to the rest rooms in back. Somewhere a radio turned low was playing one of those frantic Mediterranean melodies that sound like hornets set loose in the string section.

The waitress was freshening my coffee when my host arrived, extending a small right hand and a smiling observation on downtown Detroit traffic. Constantine Xanthes was a wiry five feet and ninety pounds with deep laugh lines from his narrow eyes to his broad mouth and hair as black at 50 as mine was going gray at 33. His light blue tailormade suit fit him like a sheen of water. He smiled a lot, but so does every other restaurateur, and none of them means it either. When he found out I hadn't eaten he ordered egg lemon soup, bread, feta cheese, roast lamb, and a bottle of ouzo for us both. I passed on the ouzo.

"Greektown used to be more than just fine places to eat." He sighed, poking a fork at his lamb. "When my parents came it was a little Athens, with markets and pretty girls in red and white dresses at festival time and noise like I can't describe to you. It took in Macomb, Randolph, and Monroe Streets, not just one block of Monroe like now. Now those colorful old men you see drinking retsina on the stoops get up and go home to the suburbs at dark."

I washed down the last of the strong cheese with coffee. "I'm a good P.I., Mr. Xanthes, but I'm not good enough to track down and bring back the old days. What else can I do to make your life easier?"

He refilled his glass with ouzo and I watched his Adam's apple bob twice as the syrupy liquid slid down his throat. Afterward he was still smiling, but the vertical line that had appeared between his brows when he was talking about what had happened to his neighborhood had deepened.

"I have a half brother, Alexander," he began. "He's twenty-three years younger than I am; his mother was our father's second wife. She deserted them when Alexander was six. When Father died, my wife and I took over the job of raising Alexander, but by then I was working sixty hours a week at General Motors and he was seventeen and too much for Grace to handle with two children of our own. He ran away. We didn't hear from him until last summer, when he walked into the house unannounced, all smiles and hugs, at least for me. He and Grace never got along. He congratulated me on my success in the restaurant business and said he'd been living in Iowa for the past nine years, where he'd married and divorced twice. His first wife left him without so much as a note and had a lawyer send him papers six weeks later. The second filed suit on grounds of brutality. It seems that during quarrels he took to beating her with the cord from an iron. He was proud of that.

"He's been here fourteen months, and in that time he's held more jobs than I can count. Some he quit, some he was fired from, always for the same reason. He can't work with or for a woman. I kept him on here as a busboy until he threw a stool at one of my waitresses. She'd asked him to get a can of coffee from the storeroom and forgot to say please. I had to let him go."

He paused, and I lit a Winston to keep from having to say anything. It was all beginning to sound familiar. I wondered why.

When he saw I wasn't going to comment, he drew a folded clipping from an inside breast pocket and spread it out on the table with the reluctant care of a father getting ready to punish his child. It was from that morning's *Free Press,* and it was headed PSYCHIATRIST PROFILES FIVE O'CLOCK STRANGLER.

That was the name the press had hung on the nut who had stalked and murdered four women on their way home from work on the city's northwest side on four separate evenings over the past two weeks. The women were found strangled to death in public places around quitting time, or reported missing by their families from that time and discovered later. Their ages ranged from 20 to 46, they had had no connection in life, and they were all WASPs. One was a nurse, two were secretaries; the fourth had been something mysterious in city government. None was raped. The Freep had dug up a shrink who claimed the killer was between 25 and 40, a member of an ethnic or racial minority group, and a hater of professional women who had had experiences with such women unpleasant enough to unhinge him. It was the kind of article you usually find in the Science section after someone's made off with Sports and the comics, only today it had run Page One because there hadn't been any murders in a couple of days to keep the story alive. I'd read it at breakfast. I knew now what had nagged me about Xanthes' story.

"Your brother's the Five O'Clock Strangler?" I tipped half an inch of ash into the tin tray on the table.

"Half brother," he corrected. "If I was sure of that, I wouldn't have called you. Alexander could have killed that waitress, Mr. Walker. As it was he nearly broke her arm with that stool and I had to pay for x rays and give her a bonus to keep her from pressing charges. This article says the strangler hates working women. Alexander hates *all* women, but working women especially. His mother was a licensed practical nurse and she abandoned him. His first wife was a legal secretary and *she* left him. He told me he started beating his second wife when she started talking about getting a job. The police say that because the killer strangles women with just his hands he has to be big and strong. That description fits my half brother; he's built more like you than me, and he works out regularly."

"Does he have anything against white Anglo-Saxon Protestants?"

"I don't know. But his mother was one and so was his first wife. The waitress he hurt was of Greek descent."

I burned some more tobacco. "Does he have an alibi for any of the times the women were killed?"

"I asked him, in a way that wouldn't make him think I suspected him. He said he was home alone." He shifted his weight on the bench. "I didn't want to press it, but I called him one of those nights and he didn't answer. But it wasn't until I read this article that I really started to worry. It could have been written about Alexander. That's when I decided to call you. You once dug up an eyewitness to an auto accident whose testimony saved a friend of mine a bundle. He talks about you often."

"I have a license to stand in front of," I said. "If your half brother *is* the strangler I'll have to send him over."

"I understand that. All I ask is that you call me before you call the police. It's this not knowing, you know? And don't let him find out he's being investigated. There's no telling what he'll do if he learns I suspect him."

We took care of finances — in cash; you'll look in vain for a checkbook in Greektown — and he slid over a wallet-size photo of a darkly handsome man in his late twenties with glossy black hair like Xanthes' and big liquid eyes not at all like Xanthes' slits. "He goes by Alex Santine. You'll find him working part-time at Butsukitis' market on Brush." A telephone number and an address on Gratiot were written on the back of the picture. That was a long way from the area where the bodies were found, but then a killer hardly ever lives in the neighborhood where he works. Not that that made any difference to the cops busy tossing every house and apartment on the northwest side.

2

He looked like his picture. After leaving the restaurant, I'd walked around the corner to a building with a fruit and vegetable stand out front and a faded canvas awning lettered BUTSU-KITIS' FINE PRODUCE, and while a beefy bald man with fat quilting his chest dropped some onions into a paper sack for me, a tall young man came out the front door lugging a crate full of cabbages. He hoisted the crate onto a bare spot on the stand, swept large shiny eyes over the milling crowd of tomato-squeezers and melon-huggers, and went back inside swinging his broad shoulders.

As the grocer was ringing up the sale, a blonde wearing a navy blue business suit asked for help loading two bags of apples and cherries into her car. "Santine!" he bellowed.

The young man returned. Told to help the lady, he hesitated, then slouched forward and snatched up the bags. He stashed them on the front seat of a green Olds parked half a block down the street and swung around and walked away while she was still rummaging in her handbag for a tip. His swagger going back into the store was pronounced. I paid for my onions and left.

Back at the office I called Iowa Information and got two

numbers. The first belonged to a private detective agency in Des Moines. I called them, fed them the dope I had on Santine, and asked them to scrape up what they could. My next call was to the Des Moines *Register,* where a reporter held me up for fifty dollars for combing the morgue for stories about non-rape female assault and murder during the last two years Santine lived in the state. They both promised to wire the information to Barry Stackpole at the Detroit *News* and I hung up and dialed Barry's number and traded a case of Scotch for his cooperation. The expenses on this one were going to eat up my fee. Finally I called Lieutenant John Alderdyce at Police Headquarters.

"Who's working the Five O'Clock Strangler case?" I asked him.

"Why?"

I used the dead air counting how many times he'd asked me that and dividing it by how many times I'd answered.

"DeLong," he said then. "I could just hang up because I'm busy, but you'd probably just call again."

"Probably. Is he in?"

"He's in that lot off Lahser where they found the last body. With Michael Kurof."

"The psychic?"

"No, the plumber. They're stopping there on their way to fix DeLong's toilet." He broke the connection.

3

The last body had been found lying in a patch of weeds in a wooded lot off Lahser just south of West Grand River by a band student taking a shortcut home from practice. I parked next to the curb behind a blue-and-white and mingled with a group of uniforms and obvious plainclothesmen watching

Kurof walk around with Inspector DeLong nipping along at his side like a spaniel trying to keep up with a Great Dane. DeLong was a razor-faced twenty-year cop with horns of pink scalp retreating along a mouse-colored widow's peak and the kind of crossed eyes that kept you wondering where he was looking. Kurof, a Russian-born bear of a man, bushy-haired and blue of chin even when it was still wet from shaving, bobbed his big head in time with DeLong's mile-a-minute patter for a few moments, then raised a palm, cutting him off. After that they wandered the lot in silence.

"What they looking for, rattlesnakes?" muttered a grizzled fatty in a baggy brown suit.

"Vibes," someone answered. "Emanations, the Russky calls 'em."

Lardbottom snorted. "We ran *in* fortune-tellers when I was in uniform."

"That must've been before you needed a crowbar to get into one," said the other.

I was nudged by a young black in starched blue cotton, who winked gravely and stooped to lay a gold pencil on the ground, then backed away from it. Kurof's back was turned. Eventually he and DeLong made their way to the spot, where the psychic picked up the pencil, stroked it once between the first and second fingers of his right hand, and turned to the black cop with a broad smile, holding out the item. "You are having fun with me, Officer," he announced in a deep burring voice. The uniform smiled stiffly back and accepted the pencil.

"Did you learn anything, Dr. Kurof?" DeLong was facing the psychic, but his right eye was looking toward the parked cars.

Kurof shook his great head slowly. "Nothing useful, I fear. Just a tangible hatred. The air is ugly everywhere here, but it is ugliest where we are standing. It crawls."

"We're standing precisely where the body was found." The

inspector pushed aside a clump of thistles with his foot to expose a fresh yellow stake driven into the earth. He turned toward one of the watching uniforms. "Give our guest a lift back to Wayne State. Thank you, Doctor. We'll be in touch when something else comes up." They shook hands and the Russian moved off slowly with his escort.

"Hatred," the fat detective growled. "Like we needed a gypsy to tell us that."

DeLong told him to shut up and go back to Headquarters. As the knot of investigators loosened, I approached the inspector and introduced myself.

"Walker," he considered. "Sure, I see you jawing with Alderdyce. Who hired you, the family of one of the victims?"

"Just running an errand." Sometimes it's best to let a cop keep his notions. "What about what this psychiatrist said about the strangler in this morning's Freep? You agree with that?"

"Shrinks. Twenty years in school to tell us why some j.d. sapped an old lady and snatched her purse. I'll stick with guys like Kurof, at least he's not smug." He stuck a Tiparillo in his mouth and I lit it and a Winston for me. He sucked smoke. "My theory is the killer's unemployed and he sees all these women running out and getting themselves fulfilled by taking his job and something snaps. It isn't just coincidence that the stats on crime against women have risen with their number in the work force."

"Is he a minority?"

"I hope so." He grinned quickly and without mirth. "No, I know what you mean. Maybe. Minorities outnumber the majority in this town in case you haven't noticed. Could be the victims are all WASPs because there are more women working who are WASPs. I'll ask him when we arrest him."

"Think you will?"

He glared at me in his cockeyed fashion. Then he shrugged. "This is the third mass-murder case I've investigated. The one fear is that it'll just stop. I'm still hoping to wrap it before famous criminologists start coming in from all over to give us a hand. I never liked circuses even when I was a kid.''

"What are you holding back from the press on this one?"

"You expect me to answer that? Give up the one thing that'll help us separate the original from all the copycats?''

"Call John Alderdyce. He'll tell you I sit on things till they hatch.''

"Oh, hell.'' He dropped his little cigar half-smoked and crushed it out. "The guy clobbers his victims before he strangles them. One blow to the left cheek, probably with his right fist. Keeps 'em from struggling.''

"Could he be a boxer?"

"Maybe. Someone used to using his dukes.''

I thanked him for talking to me. He said, "I hope you *are* working for the family of a victim.''

I got out of there without answering. Lying to a cop like DeLong can be like trying to smuggle a bicycle through Customs.

4

It was coming up on two o'clock. If the killer was planning to strike that day I had three hours. At the first telephone booth I came to I excavated my notebook and called Constantine Xanthes' home number in Royal Oak. His wife answered. She had a mellow voice and no accent.

"Yes, Connie told me he was going to hire you. He's not home, though. Try the restaurant.''

I explained she was the one I wanted to speak with and asked if I could come over. After a brief pause she agreed and gave me directions. I told her to expect me in half an hour.

It was a white frame house that would have been in the country when it was built, but now it was shouldered by two housing tracts with a third going up in the empty field across the street. The doorbell was answered by a tall woman on the far side of 40 with black hair streaked blond to cover the gray and a handsome oval face, the flesh shiny around the eyes and mouth from recent remodeling. She wore a dark knit dress that accentuated the slim line of her torso and a long colored scarf to make you forget she was big enough to look down at the top of her husband's head without trying. We exchanged greetings and she let me in and hung up my hat and we walked into a dim living room furnished heavily in oak and dark leather. We sat down facing each other in a pair of horsehair-stuffed chairs.

"You're not Greek," I said.

"I hardly ever am." Her voice was just as mellow in person.

"Your husband was mourning the old Greektown at lunch and now I find out he lives in the suburbs with a woman who isn't Greek."

"Connie's ethnic standards are very high for other people."

She was smiling when she said it, but I didn't press the point. "He says you and Alexander have never been friendly. In what ways weren't you friendly when he was living here?"

"I don't suppose it's ever easy bringing up someone else's son. His having been deserted didn't help. Lord save me if I suggested taking out the garbage."

"Was he sullen, abusive, what?"

"Sullen was his best mood. 'Abusive' hardly describes his reaction to the simplest request. The children were beginning to repeat his foul language. I was relieved when he ran away."

"Did you call the police?"

"Connie did. They never found him. By that time he was eighteen and technically an adult. He couldn't have been brought back without his consent anyway."

"Did he ever hit you?"

"He wouldn't dare. He worshiped Connie."

"Did he ever box?"

"You mean fight? I think so. Sometimes he came home from

school with his clothes torn or a black eye, but he wouldn't talk about it. That was before he quit. Fighting is normal. We had some of the same problems with our son. He grew out of it."

I was coming to the short end. "Any scrapes with the law? Alexander, I mean."

She shook her head. Her eyes were warm and tawny. "You know, you're quite good-looking. You have noble features."

"So does a German Shepherd."

"I work in clay. I'd like to have you pose for me in my studio sometime." She waved long nails toward a door to the left. "I specialize in nudes."

"So do I. But not with clients' wives." I rose.

She lifted penciled eyebrows. "Was I that obvious?"

"Probably not, but I'm a detective." I thanked her and got my hat and let myself out.

5

Xanthes had told me his half brother got off at four. At ten to, I swung by the market and bought two quarts of strawberries. The beefy bald man, whom I'd pegged as Butsukitis, the owner, appeared glad to see me. Memories are long in Greektown. I said, "I just had an operation and the doc says I shouldn't lift any more than a pound. Could your boy carry these to the car?"

"I let my boy leave early. Slow day. I will carry them."

He did, and I drove away stuck with two quarts of strawberries. They give me hives. Had Santine been around I'd planned to tail him after he punched out. Pounding the steering wheel at red lights, I bucked and squirmed my way through late afternoon traffic to Gratiot, where my man kept an apartment on the second floor of a charred brick building that had housed a recording studio in the gravy days of

Motown. I ditched my hat, jacket, and tie in the car and at Santine's door put on a pair of aviator's glasses in case he remembered me from the market. If he answered my knock I was looking for another apartment. There was no answer. I considered slipping the latch and taking a look around inside, but it was too early in the round to play catch with my license. I went back down and made myself uncomfortable in my heap across the street from the entrance.

It was growing dark when a cab creaked its brakes in front of the building and Santine got out, wearing a blue Windbreaker over the clothes I'd seen him in earlier. He paid the driver and went inside. Since the window of his apartment looked out on Gratiot I let the cab go, noting its number, hit the starter and wound my way to the company's headquarters on Woodward.

A puffy-faced black man in work clothes looked at me from behind a steel desk in an office smelling of oil. The floor tingled with the swallowed bellowing of engines in the garage below. I gave him a hinge at my investigator's photostat, placing my thumb over the "Private," and told him in an official voice I wanted information on Cab No. 218.

He looked back down at the ruled pink sheet he was scribbling on and said, "I been dispatcher here eleven years. You think I don't know a plastic badge when I see one?"

I licked a ten-dollar bill across the sheet.

"That's Dillard," he said, watching the movement.

"He just dropped off a fare on Gratiot." I gave him the address. "I want to know where he picked him up and when."

He found the cab number on another ruled sheet attached to a clipboard on the wall and followed the line with his finger to some writing in another column. "Evergreen, between Schoolcraft and Kendall. Dillard logged it in at six-twenty."

I handed him the bill without comment. The spot where Santine had entered the cab was an hour's easy walk from where the bodies of two of the murdered women had been found.

6

I swung past Alex Santine's apartment near Greektown on my way home. There was a light on. That night after supper I caught all the news reports on TV and looked for bulletins and wound up watching a succession of sitcoms full of single mothers shrieking at their kids about sex. There was nothing about any new stranglings. I went to bed. Eating breakfast next day I turned on the radio and read the *Free Press* and there was still nothing.

The name of the psychiatrist quoted in the last issue was Kornecki. I looked him up and called his office in the National Bank Building. I expected a secretary, but I got him.

"I'd like to talk to you about someone I know," I said.

"Someone you know. I see." He spoke in cathedral tones.

"It's not me. I have an entirely different set of neuroses."

"My consultation fee is one hundred dollars for forty minutes."

"I'll take twenty-five dollars' worth," I said.

"No, that's for forty minutes or any fraction thereof. I have a cancellation at eleven. Shall I have my secretary pencil you in when she returns from her break?"

I told him to do so, gave him my name, and rang off before I could say anything about his working out of a bank. The hundred went onto the expense sheet.

Kornecki's reception room was larger than my office and a half. A redhead at a kidney-shaped desk smiled tightly at me, found my name on her calendar, and buzzed me through. The inner sanctum, pastel green with a blue carpet, dark green Naugahyde couch, and a large glass-topped desk bare but for a telephone intercom, looked out on downtown through a window whose double panes swallowed the traffic noise. Behind the desk, a man about my age, wearing a blue pinstripe and steel-rimmed glasses, sat smiling at me with several thousand dollars' worth of dental work. He wore his sandy hair in bangs like Alfalfa.

We shook hands and I took charge of the customer's chair, a pedestal job upholstered in green vinyl to match the couch. I asked if I could smoke. He said whatever made me comfortable and indicated a smoking stand nearby. I lit up and laid out Santine's background without naming him. Kornecki listened.

"Is this guy capable of violence against strange women?" I finished.

He smiled again. "We all are, Mr. Walker. Every one of us men. It's our only advantage. You think your man is the strangler, is that it?"

"I guess I was absent the day they taught subtle."

"Oh, you were subtle. But you can't know how many people I've spoken with since that article appeared, wanting to be assured that their uncle or cousin or best friend isn't the killer. Hostility between the sexes is nothing new, but these last few confusing years have aggravated things. From what you've told me, though, I don't think you need to worry."

Those rich tones rumbling up from his slender chest made you want to look around to see who was talking. I waited, smoking.

"The powder is there," he went on. "But it needs a spark. If your man were to start murdering women, his second wife would have been his first victim. He wouldn't have stopped at beating her. My own theory, which the *Free Press* saw fit not to print, is that the strangler suffered some real or imagined wrong at a woman's hand in his past, and that recently the wrong was repeated, either by a similar act committed by another woman, or by his coming into contact with the same woman."

"What sort of wrong?"

"It could be anything. Sexual domination is the worst, because it means loss of self-esteem. Possibly she worked for a living, but it's just as likely that he equates women who work with her dominance. They would be a substitute; he would lack the courage to strike out at the actual source of his frustration."

"Suppose he ran into his mother or something like that."

He shook his head. "Too far back. I don't place as much importance on early childhood as many of my colleagues. Stale charges don't explode that easily."

"You've been a big help," I said, and we talked about sports and politics until my hundred dollars were up.

7

From there I went to the Detroit *News* and Barry Stackpole's cubicle, where he greeted me with the lopsided grin the steel plate in his head had left him with after some rough trade tried to blow him up in his car, and pointed to a stack of papers on his desk. I sat on one of the antique whiskey crates he uses to file things in — there was a similar stack on the only other chair besides his — and went through the stuff. It had come over the wire that morning from the Des Moines agency and the *Register,* and none of it was for me. Santine had held six jobs in his last two years in Iowa, fetch-and-carry work, no brains need apply. His first wife had divorced him on grounds of marriage breakdown and he hadn't contested the action. His second had filed for extreme cruelty. The transcripts of that one were ugly but not uncommon. There were enough articles from the newspaper on violent crimes against women to make you think twice before moving there, but if there was a pattern it was lost on me. The telephone rang while I was reshuffling the papers. Barry barked his name into the receiver, paused, and held it out to me.

"I gave my service this number," I explained, accepting it.

"You bastard, you promised to call me before you called the police."

The voice belonged to Constantine Xanthes. I straightened. "Start again."

"Alexander just called me from Police Headquarters. They've arrested him for the stranglings."

8

I met Xanthes in Homicide. He was wearing the same light blue suit or one just like it and his face was pale beneath the olive pigment. "He's being interrogated now," he said stiffly. "My lawyer's with him."

"I didn't call the cops." I made my voice low. The room was alive with uniforms and detectives in shirtsleeves droning into telephones and comparing criminal anecdotes at the water cooler.

"I know. When I got here, Inspector DeLong told me Alexander walked into some kind of trap."

On cue, DeLong entered the squad room from the hallway leading to Interrogation. His jacket was off and his shirt clung transparent to his narrow chest. When he saw me his cross-eyes flamed. "You said you were representing a *victim's* family."

"I didn't," I said. "You did. What's this trap?"

He grinned to his molars. "It's the kind of thing you do in these things when you did everything else. Sometimes it works. We had another strangling last night."

My stomach took a dive. "It wasn't on the news."

"We didn't release it. The body was found jammed into a culvert on Schoolcraft. When we got the squeal we threw wraps over it, morgued the corpse — she was a teacher at Redford High — and stuck a department-store dummy in its place. These nuts like publicity; when there isn't any they might check to see if the body is still there. Nick the Greek in there climbs down the bank at half-past noon and takes a look inside and three officers step out of the bushes and screw their service revolvers in his ears."

"Pretty thin," I said.

"How thick does it have to be with a full confession?"

Xanthes swayed. I grabbed his arm. I was still looking at DeLong.

"He's talking to a tape recorder now," he said, filling a Dixie cup at the cooler. "He knows the details on all five murders, including the blow to the cheek."

"I'd like to see him." Xanthes was still pale, but he wasn't needing me to hold him up now.

"It'll be a couple of hours."

"I'll wait."

The inspector shrugged, drained the cup, and headed back the way he'd come, sidearming the crumpled container at a steel wastebasket already bubbling over with them. Xanthes said, "He didn't do it."

"I think he probably did." I was somersaulting a Winston back and forth across the back of my hand. "Is your wife home?"

He started slightly. "Grace? She's shopping for art supplies in Southfield. I tried to reach her after the police called, but I couldn't."

"I wonder if I could have a look at her studio."

"Why?"

"I'll tell you in the car." When he hesitated: "It beats hanging around here."

He nodded. In my crate I said, "Your father was proud of his Greek heritage, wasn't he?"

"Fiercely. He was a stonecutter in the old country and built like Hercules. He taught me the importance of being a man and the sanctity of womanhood. That's why I can't understand . . ." He shook his head, watching the scenery glide past his window.

"I can. When a man who's been told all his life that a man should be strong lets himself be humiliated by a woman it does things to him. If he's smart he'll put distance between himself and the woman. If he's weak he'll come back and it'll start all over again. And if the woman happens to be married to his half brother, who he worships —"

I stopped, feeling the flinty chips of his eyes on me. "Who told you that?"

"Your wife, some of it. You, some more. The rest of it I got from a psychiatrist downtown. The women's movement has changed the lives of almost everyone but the women who have the most to lose by embracing it. Your wife's been cheating on you for years."

"Liar!" He lunged across the seat at me. I spun the wheel hard and we shrieked around a corner and he slammed back against the passenger's door. A big Mercury that had been close on our tail blatted its horn and sped past. Xanthes breathed heavily, glaring.

"She propositioned me like a pro yesterday." I corrected our course. We were entering his neighborhood now. "I think she's been doing that kind of thing a long time. I think that when he was living at your place Alexander found out and threatened to tell you. That would have meant divorce from a proud man like you, and your wife would have had to go to work to support herself and the children. So she bribed Alexander with the only thing she had to bribe him with. She's still attractive, but in those days she must have been a knockout; being weak, he took the bribe, and then she had leverage. She hedged her bet by making up those stories about his incorrigible behavior so that you wouldn't believe him if he did tell you. So he got out from under. But the experience had plundered him of his self-respect and tainted his relationships with women from then on. Even then he might have grown out of it, but he made the mistake of coming back. Seeing her again shook something loose. He walked into your house Alex Santine and came out the Five O'Clock Strangler, victimizing seemingly independent WASP women like Grace. Who taught him how to use his fists?"

"Our father, probably. He taught me. It was part of a man's

training, he said, to know how to defend himself." His voice was as dead as last year's leaves.

We pulled into his driveway and he got out, moving very slowly. Inside the house we paused before the locked door to his wife's studio. I asked him if he had a key.

"No. I've never been inside the room. She's never invited me and I respect her privacy."

I didn't. I slipped the lock with the edge of my investigator's photostat and we entered Grace Xanthes' trophy room.

It had been a bedroom, but she had erected steel utility shelves and moved in a kiln and a long library table on which stood a turning pedestal supporting a lump of red clay that was starting to look like a naked man. The shelves were lined with nude male figure studies twelve to eighteen inches high, posed in various heroic attitudes. They were all of a type, athletically muscled and wide at the shoulders, physically large, all the things the artist's husband wasn't. He walked around the room in a kind of daze, staring at each in turn. It was clear he recognized some of them. I didn't know Alexander at first, but he did. He had filled out since 17.

9

I returned two days' worth of Xanthes' three-day retainer, less expenses, despite his insistence that I'd earned it. A few weeks later, court-appointed psychiatrists declared Alex Santine mentally unfit to stand trial and he was remanded for treatment to the State Forensics Center at Ypsilanti. And I haven't had a bowl of egg lemon soup or a slice of feta cheese in months.

Robbers' Roost

I WAS MET at the door by a hatchet-faced woman in a nurse's uniform who took my card and asked me to accompany her to Dr. Tuskin's office. I hadn't come to see anyone by that name, but I said okay. I have another set of manners when my checks don't bounce. On the way we passed some old people in wheelchairs whose drugged eyes followed us the way the eyes of sunning lizards follow visitors to the zoo. The place was a nursing home for the aged.

"I can't let you see Mr. Chubb," announced Dr. Tuskin, after we had shaken hands and the nature of my visit was established. The nurse had withdrawn. "Perhaps I can help you, Mister" — he glanced down at my card — "Walker?"

He was tall and plump with very white hair and wore a three-piece suit the color of creamed anything. His office wore a lot of cedar and the desk he was standing behind was big and glossy and bare but for the card. I didn't think he'd scooped any paperwork into a drawer on my account.

"I doubt it," I said. "I got a telephone call from Mr. Chubb requesting my services. If he hasn't confided in you we've nothing to discuss."

"He is infirm. I can't imagine what reasons he'd have for engaging a private investigator at this time in his life." But his frost-blue eyes were uneasy. I played on that.

"I don't think they have anything to do with the operation of this home or he wouldn't have made the call from one of your telephones." I dropped the reassuring tone. "But I have

a friend on the *News* who might be interested in finding out
why a private investigator was denied access to one of your
patients.''

His face tightened. "That sounds like blackmail.''

"I was hoping it would.''

After a moment he pressed something under his desk. Reap-
pearing, Hatchet Face was instructed to take me to Oscar
Chubb's room on the second floor. Dr. Tuskin didn't say
good-bye as we left.

Upstairs lay a very old man in bed, his pale, hollow-templed
head almost lost amidst the pillow and heavy white quilt. The
nurse awakened him gently, told him who I was, and moved to
draw the blinds over the room's only window, which looked
out over the choppy blue-green surface of Lake St. Clair.

"Leave it,'' he bleated. "It's taken me eighty years to get to
Grosse Pointe. I like to be reminded.''

She went out, muttering something about the glare and his
cataract.

"As if it mattered.'' He mined a bony arm in a baggy pajama
sleeve out from under the heavy spread, rested it a moment,
then used the remote control atop the spread to raise himself
to a sitting position. He waved me into the chair next to the
bed.

"I hear you're good.''

"Good's a pretty general term,'' I said. "I'm good in some
areas. Missing persons, yeah. Divorce, no. I have a low gag
threshold.''

"Have you ever heard of Specs Kleinstein?''

"Racketeer. Retired, lives in Troy.''

He nodded feebly. His eyes were swollen in the shriveled
face and his head quaked. "I want him in jail.''

"You, the Detroit Police, and the FBI.'' I stuck a cigarette in
my mouth, then remembered where I was, and started to put it
away. He told me to go ahead and smoke. I said, "Sure?''

"Don't worry about killing me. I'm hardier than I look.''

"You'd almost have to be.''

He smiled, or tried to. The corners of his lipless mouth tugged out a tenth of an inch. "You remind me of Eddie."

"Eddie?" I lit up.

"He's the reason I want Specs behind bars. The reason you're here. You know about Robbers' Roost?"

I blew smoke away from the bed. "If I answer this one right, do I get the range or the trip to Hawaii?"

"Indulge my senility. You won't find the Roost on any map, but if you ask any old-time Detroiter about it he'll grin and give you directions a blind man could follow. It covers ten blocks along the river in Ecorse where rumrunners from Canada used to dock during Prohibition. Eddie and I grew up there."

"Eddie was your brother?"

"Yes and no. His last name was Stoner. My folks adopted him in nineteen twelve after his folks were killed in a streetcar accident on Woodward. You ever see an old Warner Brothers picture called *Angels with Dirty Faces?*"

"A time or twelve."

"Well, it was Eddie and me right on the button. We were the same age, but he grew up faster on account of a four-alarm temper and a pair of fists like pistons. When college time came and my parents could afford to send only one of us, it was Eddie who stepped aside. After graduation I joined the Ecorse Police Department. Eddie got a job delivering bootleg hooch for Specs Kleinstein.

"I asked him how far he thought I'd get in the force when it got out that I had Mob connections. He said, 'Probably chief,' and I knocked him down for the first and only time in my life. He moved out soon after."

Chubb closed his eyes. Whatever breathing he was doing wasn't enough to stir the quilt over his chest. But his nostrils were quivering and I relaxed.

"One day I pulled over a big gray Cadillac for running a stop sign on Jefferson," he went on. "Eddie was behind the wheel with a girl in the passenger's seat and ten cases of Old Log

Cabin stacked in back. The girl was Clara Baxter, Kleinstein's mistress. Eddie laughed when I told him to watch his butt. Well, I took them in, car and all. They were back on the street an hour later with everything returned, including the liquor. That was how things worked back then."

"Back then." I flicked some ash into a pantscuff.

Chubb ignored the comment. "I never saw him again. That winter the river froze over, and the boats went into drydock while old cars were used to ferry the stuff across. I still have the clipping."

A yellow knuckle twitched at the bedstand. In the drawer was a square of brown newsprint fifty years old. BOOTLEGGER DIES AS ICE COLLAPSES, bellowed the headline. I read swiftly.

"It says it was an accident," I said. "The ice gave way under Stoner's car and he went to the bottom."

"Yeah. It was just coincidence that Specs found out about Eddie stealing his woman the day before the accident and threatened to kill him. I have that on good authority."

"You tried to nail him for it?"

"For thirty-two years, until retirement. No evidence."

"What made you decide to try again now?"

He opened his huge eyes and turned them on me. "In confidence?"

I nodded.

"This morning I had a little stroke. I still can't grip anything with my right hand. Nobody here even knows about it. But I won't survive another."

I smoked and thought. "I wouldn't know where to start after all this time."

"You do if your recommendation is any good. Try Walter Barnes in Ecorse. He was my partner for fourteen years and he knows as much about the case as I do. Then you might see what you can do about recovering Eddie's remains."

"He's still down there?"

"I never could get the city to pay out to raise a gangster's body. The car isn't a hazard to navigation."

I folded away the clipping inside my jacket and stood. "My fee's two-fifty a day plus expenses."

"See my son. His number's on the back of the clipping."

"Be seeing you."

"Don't count on it."

2

I found Walter Barnes watering the lawn of his brick split-level on Sunnyside, a tall man in his early seventies with pinkish hair thinning in front and a paunch that strained the buttons on his fuzzy green sweater. He wore a hearing aid, so naturally I started the interview at the top of my lungs.

"Stop shouting or I'll spray you," he snapped. "Who'd you say you were?"

I handed him my card. He moved his lips as he read.

"Amos Walker, huh? Never heard of you."

"You're in the majority. What can you tell me about Eddie Stoner?"

"Who'd you say you're working for?" His eyes were narrow openings in thickets of wrinkles.

"Oscar Chubb. You used to be partners."

His face softened. "Oscar. How is he?"

"Dying."

"I been hearing that for ten years. Who was it you asked me about?"

"Eddie Stoner." I made strangling motions with my hands in my pockets.

His lips drew back over his dentures. "Eddie was bad. He was the reason Oscar took so long getting his stripes. The brass didn't like having a hoodlum's brother on the force, blood kin or no."

"Tell me about Eddie's death."

His story was loaded with repetitions and back-telling, but I gathered that it was one of Barnes's snitches who had carried the tale of Kleinstein's death threat. Clara Baxter had blurted out the details of her fling during an argument. A scuffle with Eddie followed; Kleinstein's eyeglasses got broken along with his nose, and he sputtered through the blood that Stoner wouldn't see Thursday.

"Way I see it," the ex-cop wrapped up, "Specs wormed his way back into Eddie's confidence somehow, then let him have it in the car that night on the ice. Then he got out a spud and chopped a circle around the car so it broke through, and headed back on foot. But we never could prove they were together that night."

"What happened to Clara Baxter?"

"She left town right after the fight. Last I heard she was back and living in Detroit. Married some guy named Fix or Wicks, something like that. I heard he died. Hell, her too, probably, by now."

"Thanks, Mr. Barnes. Who do I see about fishing Eddie's remains out of the river?"

He turned off the nozzle and started rolling up the hose with slow, deliberate movements of his spotted hands. "In this town, no one. Money's too tight to waste solving a murder no one cares about anymore."

"I hope you're wrong, Mr. Barnes," I said. "About no one caring, I mean."

He made no reply. For all I knew, his hearing aid needed fresh batteries.

3

A Clara Wicks and two C. Fixes were listed in the Detroit directory. I tried them from my office. The first was a thirty-year-old divorcée who tried to rape me over the telephone and the others were men. Then I got tricky and dialed the number for C. Hicks. No answer. Next I rang Lieutenant John Alder-dyce on Detroit Homicide, who owed me a favor. He collected on a poker debt from a cop on the Ecorse Police, whose wife's brother knew a member of the city council, who had something on the mayor. Half an hour later Alderdyce called back to say that dragging for the submerged car would start first thing in the morning. Democracy is a system of checks and balances.

There was still no answer at the Hicks number. The house was on Livernois. I thought I'd check it out, and had my hand on the door handle of my war-torn Cutlass when two guys crowded in on either side of me. Together they'd have filled Tiger Stadium.

"You got a previous engagement, chum," said the one on my left, a black with scar tissue over both eyes and a sagging lower lip that left his bottom teeth exposed. His partner wasn't as pretty.

I was hustled into the rear of a dark blue Lincoln in the next slot down, where Gorgeous sat next to me while the other drove. After that the conversation lagged.

Kleinstein was leaning on a cane in the living room of his Troy townhouse when we entered. His white hair was fine over shiny scalp and his neck and hands were spotted, but aside from that he was the Specs whose picture I'd seen in books about Prohibition, down to the thick eyeglasses that had earned him his nickname. He had on a pastel blue sport shirt and gray trousers with pleats.

"You're working for Oscar Chubb." His Yiddish accent was faint but there. "Why?"

"I'm supporting a habit. I have to eat every now and then."

His cane slashed upward. A black light burst inside my temple. I reeled, then lurched forward, but the gargoyles who had brought me stepped between us. Unarmed that day, I relaxed.

"Next time don't be flip," warned the old man. "What've you found out?"

"If you hit me with that cane again I'll make you eat it."

Gorgeous lumbered toward me, dropping one shoulder. I

pivoted and kicked. The side of my sole met his kneecap with an audible snap. Howling, he grasped it and staggered backward until he fell into an overstuffed chair. He started to blubber. His partner roared and lunged, but Kleinstein smacked the cane across his chest, halting him.

"All right, you're a hardcase. The cemetery's full of them. Some guys are just too dumb to scare. You're here because I want you to know I didn't kill Stoner."

"Who told you I cared?"

He smiled dryly. The spectacles magnified his eyes to three times their normal size. "Let's stick to the subject. Five witnesses swore I was nowhere near the river that night."

"My client says different."

"Your client is senile."

"Maybe. We'll know for sure tomorrow. The City of Ecorse is raising the car Stoner died in."

He didn't turn pale or try to walk on the ceiling. I hadn't really expected him to. "How much evidence do you think they'll find after fifty years?" He flushed. "Look at this house, Walker. I've lived like this a long time. Do you think I'd risk it on a cheap broad?"

"Maybe you wouldn't. The old Specs might have."

He spat on the carpet. The thug in him would always come through in moments like this. Turning to the uninjured flunky: "Take this punk back to his building and get a doctor for Richard on your way back." To me: "Step soft, Walker. Things have a way of blowing up around people I don't like."

I took him literally. When the gorilla dropped me off I checked under the hood before starting my car.

4

The Hicks home stood in a seedy neighborhood where old jalopies went to die, a once-white frame house with an attached garage and a swaybacked roof, surrounded by weeds. When no one answered my third knock I tried the door. It was unlocked.

The living room was cozy. Magazines and cheap paperbacks flung everywhere, assorted items of clothing slung over the shabby furniture and piled on the colorless rug. In the bedroom I found a single bed, unmade, and a woman's purse containing the usual junk and a driver's license in the name of Clara Hicks, aged 68. I was in the right place. A small, functional kitchen boasted an old refrigerator, a two-burner stove, and a sink and counter where a sack of groceries waited to be put away. The sack was wet. Two packages of hamburger were half thawed inside.

There was a throbbing noise behind a side door. My stomach dropped through a hole. I tore open the door and dashed into a wall of noxious smoke.

She was lying in the back seat of a six-year-old Duster with her hands folded demurely on her stomach. Her mousy gray hair was rumpled, but aside from that she was rigged for the street, in an inexpensive gray suit and floral print blouse. I recognized her sagging features from the picture on her driver's license. Coughing through my handkerchief, I reached over the seat to turn off the ignition and felt her throat for a pulse. After thirty seconds I gave up.

I climbed out and pulled up the garage door, gulped some air, then went back and steeled myself to run my fingers over her scalp. There was a sticky lump the size of a Ping-Pong ball above her left ear.

5

Two hours after I called him, I was still sitting in a chair in the kitchen talking to John Alderdyce. John's black, my age, and a spiffy dresser for a cop. In the garage they were still popping flashbulbs and picking up stray buttons.

"It could be suicide," I acknowledged. "She bought groceries today and left that hamburger thawing out in case you boys in Homicide got hungry."

The lieutenant made a disgusting noise. "That's what I can always count on from you, sincerity," he snarled. "The M.E. says she probably suffered cardiac arrest when the blow was struck, an hour or so before you found her. Who would you fit for it? Specs?"

"Maybe. I can't help wondering why, if he was going to do it, he didn't have her iced fifty years ago. The fact that I was with him about the time she took the blow means nothing. He could have had it catered. You'd better talk to Barnes."

"Not that I wasn't planning to anyway, but why?"

"Aside from Specs and Chubb, he was the only one who knew I was on the case. Someone had to tell Kleinstein."

"That opens up all sorts of unpleasant possibilities."

"Buying cops was invented in the twenties," I said. "Look up his record. Maybe he knows who dropped the contract on Eddie Stoner."

"That one's yours. I've got enough new murders on my hands. I don't have to tinker with old ones too."

I fumbled out a cigarette and stuck it between my lips without lighting it. My throat was raw from them as it was. "Someone doesn't agree with you. This particular old murder bothered him enough to make committing a new one seem worthwhile."

"Barnes is the one told you about the Baxter woman in the first place."

"He knew I'd suspect him if he didn't. He very conveniently forgot her married name, remember. Of course, I'm assuming she hasn't made enemies in the interim. That one's yours."

"Thanks. I wouldn't have known if you hadn't told me." He put away his notepad. "That'll do for now, Walker. Your help is appreciated."

I'd heard sweeter thanks from muggers. "Don't mention it.

Finding little old ladies sapped and gassed is a favorite hobby of mine."

That night I dreamed I was out swimming on a warm evening when I came upon a vintage car sunk in the mud, moonlight shining on it through the water. Peering inside, I was snatched by flabby hands and found myself grappling with an old woman whose face was blotched gray with death. We rolled over and over, but her grip was like iron and I couldn't shake her. I awoke as drenched as if I had actually been in the water.

The telephone was ringing. It was John Alderdyce.

"Good news and bad news, shamus. Sheriff's men got Barnes at Metro Airport a few minutes ago, boarding a plane for L.A."

"What's the bad news?"

"We looked up his record. There's nothing to indicate he was anything but square. I wish to hell mine were as good."

That tore it as far as getting a good night's sleep was concerned. I sat up smoking cigarettes until dawn.

6

The day was well along when Alderdyce and I shared the Ecorse dock with a crowd of local cops and the curious, watching a rusty sedan rise from the river at the end of a cable attached to a derrick on the pier. Streaming water, the glistening hulk swung in a wide, slow arc and descended to a cleared section of dock. The crane's motor died. Water hissed down the archaic vehicle's boiler-shaped cowl and puddled around the rotted tires.

Uniforms held back the crowd while John and I inspected the interior. Decayed wooden crates had tumbled over everything. Something lay on the floor in front, swaddled in rags and what remained of the upholstery. White, turtle-gnawed bone showed through the tattered and blackened fabric.

"Not much hope of proving he was sapped or shot," said the lieutenant. "The denizens of the deep have seen to that."

"Even so," I said, "having a *corpus delicti* makes for a warm, cozy feeling. Is Barnes still in custody?"

"For the time being. We won't be able to hold him much longer without evidence. What is it?"

A longshoreman who had been pressed into service to unload the cargo had exclaimed as he lifted out the first of the crates. "Awful light for a box full of booze," he said, setting it down on the dock.

A crowbar was produced and the rotted boards gave way easily to reveal nothing inside. Alderdyce directed another crate to be opened, and another. They were equally unrewarding.

"I wonder why Eddie would risk his life for a carload of empty boxes," I mused, breaking the silence.

7

In the end, it was the boxes and not the body that broke him. After an hour of questioning, Alderdyce dropped the bombshell about the strange cargo, whereupon Barnes's face lost all color and he got so tongue-tied he couldn't keep his lies straight. When he started confessing, the stenographer had to ask him twice to slow down so she could keep up.

Outside Oscar Chubb's room that evening an orderly with shoulders you couldn't hike across grasped my upper arm as I started to push past and I asked him to let go. He squeezed harder, twisting the muscle and leering. I jabbed four stiffened fingers into the arch of his ribcage. When he doubled over I snatched hold of his collar and opened the door with his head. Inside, a gentle boot in the rump laid him out on his face.

Dr. Tuskin and the hatchet-faced nurse were standing on the other side of the bed. An oxygen tent covered Chubb's head and torso and he was wired to an oscilloscope whose feeble beep disconcertingly resembled a countdown. The noise echoed the beating of my client's heart.

"Call the police," Tuskin told the nurse.

"Uh-uh." I blocked her path. "What happened?"

Tuskin hesitated. "Stroke. It happened shortly after you left yesterday. What right have you to break in and batter my staff?"

I studied the gaunt face behind transparent plastic. "Is he conscious?"

Before the doctor could respond, Chubb's eyelids rolled open and the great eyes slued my way. To Tuskin I said, "This will only take a minute. It'll be on tonight's news, so you can stay if you like."

He liked. I spoke for longer than a minute, but by then no one was watching the clock. The dying man lay with his eyes closed most of the time. I had only the peeping of the electronic whozis to tell me I still had an audience.

"I confirmed it in back issues of the *News* and *Free Press* at the library," I went on. "That wasn't the first load of hooch Specs paid for and never got. His rumrunning boats and cars had a habit of sinking and getting hijacked, more than those of his rivals. Eddie bought the stuff in Canada with the boss's money, stashed part of it to be picked up later, and saw to it that the empty crates he'd replaced it with got lost. He was making a respectable profit off each load. Kleinstein got wind of it and threatened him. Eddie and Clara never were an item. That was just Barnes's story."

Chubb's lips moved. I didn't need to hear him.

"Sure you saw them together," I said. "They were retrieving a load from one of their caches. If Barnes was Eddie's pipeline into the police department, as he's confessed, Clara was his spy in Specs's inner circle, ready to sound the alarm if he ever got suspicious. When he did, Barnes panicked and had Eddie taken out to keep him from talking.''

I read his lips again and shook my head.

"No. I thought Barnes had killed him too until we checked out his alibi. The night Eddie went down, your partner was sitting vigil in a Harper Woods funeral parlor with a cousin's remains. Two people who were with him that night are still alive, and they've confirmed it. There was only one other person who had a stake in Eddie's death, who he would have trusted to go with him that last night."

His lips didn't move this time. I hurried on.

"It was the girl, Mr. Chubb. Clara Baxter. She shot him and spent all night chipping a hole under the car to cover the evidence. Barnes hasn't changed much in fifty years. When I started poking around he lost his head again and tipped Klein-stein anonymously to get me out of the way while he offed Clara. He knew she wouldn't confess to Eddie's murder, but if Specs got suspicious and wrung the truth about the swindle out of her, Barnes was cold meat. In court he stood a chance. The underworld doesn't offer one."

I waited, but he didn't respond. After a brief examination Dr. Tuskin announced that his patient had lapsed into coma.

I never found out if he was conscious long enough to appreciate the fact that he'd spent half a century hating a man for the wrong reason. He died early the next morning without telling his son about our arrangement, and I didn't have enough capital on hand to sue his estate. But I wasn't the biggest loser by far.

Three days after his arraignment on two counts of murder, while awaiting trial in the Wayne County Jail, Walter Barnes was found strangled to death in his cell with the cord from his hearing aid. The coroner called it suicide.

Fast Burn

1

THE OLD MAN wrestled open my inner office door and held it with a shoulder while he worked his way inside, supporting himself on two steel canes, dragging one foot behind him that clanked when he let his weight down on it. He had a corrugated brow and a long loose face of that medium gray that very black skin sometimes turns with age, shot through with concentration and pain. His brown suit bagged at the knees and no two buttons on the jacket matched.

At that moment I was up to my wrists in typewriter ribbon, changing spools on the venerable Underwood portable that came with the office, and unable to get up from behind my desk to assist him — not that he looked like someone who was accustomed to receiving help from anyone. I simply said hello and nodded toward the customer's chair on his side. While I threaded the ribbon through the various forks, hooks, and prongs I heard him lower himself thankfully onto semisoft vinyl and make the little metallic snicking noises that went with undoing the braces securing the canes to his wrists.

I took my time, giving him breathing space. Going to see a private investigator isn't like visiting the dentist. I come at the desperate end of the long line of friends, relatives, friends of relatives, friends of friends, and guys around the corner whose friends owe them favors. By the time the potential client gets around to me he's admitted that his problem has grown beyond him and his circle. So I let this one resign himself to the last stop before the abyss and didn't realize until I looked up again that I was playing host to a dead man.

You know dead once you've seen it a few times, and the old man's cocked head and black open mouth with spittle hanging at one corner and the glittering crescents of his half-open eyes said it even as I got up and moved around the desk to feel his neck for an artery he didn't need any longer. His face was four shades darker than it had been coming in, and bunched like a fist. He'd suffered six kinds of hell in that last quiet moment.

I broke a pair of surgical gloves out of a package I keep in the desk, put them on, and went through his pockets. When someone dies in a room you pay rent on it's only polite to learn who he is. If the driver's license in his dilapidated wallet was valid, his name was Emmett Gooding and he lived — had lived — on Mt. Elliott near the cemetery. What a crippled old man was doing still driving was strictly between him and the Michigan Secretary of State's office. There were twelve dollars in the wallet and a ring of keys in his right pants pocket, nothing else on him except a handful of pocket lint and a once-white handkerchief that crackled when unfolded. He was wearing a steel brace on his left leg. I put everything back where I'd found it and dialed 911.

The prowl car cop who showed up ten minutes later looked about 17, with no hair on his face and no promise of it and a glossy black visor screwed down to the eyes. He put on gloves of his own to feel Gooding's neck and told me after a minute that he was dead.

"That's why I called," I said, knocking ash off a Winston into the souvenir ashtray on my desk. "I wanted a second opinion."

"You kill him?" He laid a hand on his side arm.

"I'll answer that question when it counts."

Creases marred the freckles under his eyes. "When's that?"

"Now." I nodded at the first of two plainclothesmen coming in the door. He was a slender black with a Fu Manchu moustache and coils of gray hair like steel wool at his temples, wearing the kind of electric blue suit that looks like hell on anybody but him. I knew him as Sergeant Blake, having seen him around Detroit Police Headquarters but not often enough to talk to. His companion was white, short, fifteen pounds too heavy for department regs, and a good ten years too old for active duty. He had a brush cut, jug ears, and so much upper lip it hung down over the hollow in his chin. I didn't know him from Sam's cat. You can live in a city the size of Detroit a long time and never get to know all the cops on the detective force if you're lucky.

Blake's flat eyes slid over the stiff quickly and lit on the uniform as he flashed his badge and ID. "Anything?"

"Just what's here, Sarge," reported the youngster, and handed me a glance meant to be hard. "Suspect's uncooperative."

"Okay, crash." And the uniform was off the case. When he had gone: "They're running too small to keep these days."

The short fat cop grunted.

"Amos Walker, right?" Blake looked at me for the first time. I nodded. "This is my partner, Officer Fister. Who's the dead guy?"

I said I didn't know and gave him the story, leaving out the part about searching the body. Cops consider that their province, which it is. Fister meanwhile wrapped a handkerchief around his fingers and drew the dead man's wallet out of his inside breast pocket. He had probably run out of surgical gloves years ago. He read off what mattered on the driver's license and inventoried the other contents. Blake watched me carefully while this was going on, and I made my face just as carefully blank. At length he gave a little shrug. That was it until the medical examiner arrived with his black metal case and glanced at Gooding's discolored face and looked at his fingers and took off the dead man's right shoe and sock and examined the bottom of his foot and then put all his instruments back in the case, humming to himself. He was a young Oriental. They are almost always Orientals; I think it has something to do with ancestor worship.

Blake looked at him and the M.E. said, "Massive coronary. We'll root around inside and spend a hunk of taxpayer's money on tests and it'll still come out massive coronary. When their faces turn that shade and there's evidence of an earlier stroke" — he indicated the leg brace, part of which showed under the dead man's pantsleg — "it can't be much else."

The sergeant thanked him and when the expert left had me tell the story again for Fister's notepad and then again just for fun while the white coats came to bag the body and cart it down to the wagon. "Any ideas about why he came here?" Blake asked. I shook my head. He sighed. "Okay. We might need your statement later if Charlie Chan turns out to be wrong about the heart attack."

"He didn't act like someone who's been wrong recently," I said.

Fister grunted again. "Tell me. I never met one of them croakers didn't think his sweat smelled like lilacs."

On that sparkling note they left me.

2

I spent the rest of the week tailing a state senator's aide around Lansing for his wife in Detroit, who was curious about the weekends he was spending at the office. Turned out he had a wife in the state capital, too. I was grinning my way through my typewritten report at the desk when Sergeant Blake came in. He wore a tired look and the same shocking blue suit. There couldn't be another like it in the city.

"You're off the hook," he announced. "Gooding's heart blew like the M.E. said. We checked him out. He was on the line at the Dearborn plant till he took his mandatory four years ago. Worked part-time flagging cars during road construction for County, had a stroke last year, and quit. No family. Papers in his dump on Mt. Elliott said he was getting set to check into a nursing home on Dequindre. Staff at the home expected him this week. Next to his phone we found Monday's *Free Press* folded to an article about employee theft that mentioned you as an investigator and the Yellow Pages open to the page with your number on it."

"That was a feature piece about a lot of dead cases." I stapled the report. "What did he want with me?"

"*¿Quién sabe?* Maybe he thought this was the elephant graveyard for old Ford workers. I'd care if he died any way but natural."

"Okay if I look into it?"

"Why? There's no one to stand your fee."

"He came looking for help with something. I'd like to know what it was."

"It's your time." He opened the door.

"Thanks for coming down, Sergeant. You could have called."

"I'm on my way home. I dropped off a uniform to drive Gooding's car to the impound. We found it in the lot next door."

He went out and I got up to file my carbon of the report to the woman with the generous husband. The window behind the desk started chattering, followed an instant later by a massive hollow *crump* that rang my telephone bell. At first I thought it was the ancient furnace blowing. Then I remembered it was June and got my .38 out of the desk. I almost bumped into Blake standing in the hall with his Police Special drawn. He glanced at me without saying anything and together we clattered down three flights to the street. Something that wasn't an automobile any longer squatted in a row of vehicles in the parking lot next to my building with its hood and doors sprung and balls of orange flame rolling out of its shattered windows, pouring black smoke into the smog layer overhead. Sirens keened in the distance, years too late to help the officer cooking in the front seat.

3

Shadows were congealing when I got away from Headquarters, dry-mouthed from talking to a tape recorder and damp under the arms from Sergeant Blake's enthusiastic interrogation. The bomb squad was still looking at the charred husk of Gooding's car, but it was a fair bet that a healthy charge had been rigged to the ignition. Gooding was Homicide's meat now and my permission to investigate his interest in me had died with the uniformed cop. So I called an old acquaintance in Personnel at the City-County Building from a public booth and asked for information on the old man's brief employment with the Road Commission; if I'd had brains to begin with I would have invested in two chinchillas instead of a license and waited for spring. My acquaintance promised to get back to me next day during business hours. I hung up and drove to Dearborn, where no one working the late shift at the Ford plant had ever heard of Emmett Gooding. The turnover in the auto industry is worse than McDonald's. I caught the personnel manager just as he was leaving his office, flashed my ID, and told him I was running a credit check on Gooding for a finance company. Reluctantly he agreed to go back in and pull the old man's file. The manager was small, with a shaved head and a very black pointed beard that didn't make him look anything like the high priest of the Church of Satan. He scowled at the papers in the Manila folder.

"He was a steady worker, didn't take as many sick days as you might expect from someone nearing mandatory retirement. Turned down the foreman's job twice in eighteen years. No surprise. It's a thankless position, not worth the raise."

"Is there anyone still working here who knew him?" I asked.

"Probably not. A robot's doing his job these days." He winced. "I had a computer expert in here recently bragging about how the machines free workers from inhuman jobs to explore their true potential. In my day we called it unemployment."

There was nothing in that for me, so I thanked him and got up. His eyes followed me. "What's a man Gooding's age want with a loan?"

"He's buying a hot tub," I said, and got out of there.

That was it for one day. I had a bill to make out for the bigamist's wife, and contrary to what you read, private stars don't often work at night, when most sources are closed. The bill complete, I caught a senile pork chop and a handful of wilted fries at the diner down the street from my office and went home. There was just a black spot on the parking lot pavement where Gooding's car had stood.

After breakfast the next morning I drove down to the City-County Building, making a gun out of my index finger and snapping a shot at the statue of the Spirit of Detroit on my way in. The Green Giant, as we call him, was still threatening to crush the family he was holding in one hand with the globe he was gripping in the other. The blunt instrument symbolized Progress.

I owed my contact in Personnel to having sprung his younger brother from a charge of assaulting a police officer upon producing evidence that the cop had a history of trying to pull moving violators out of their cars through the vent windows. It had cost me some good will at Police Headquarters, but the access to confidential records was worth it. My man looked like 14 trying to pass for 40, with freckles, hornrims, and short sandy hair parted with a protractor. Never mind his name.

"What you got?" I slung my frame into the treacherous scoop chair in front of his gray metal desk and lit up.

He pushed a spotless white ashtray my way. He was one of those non-smokers who didn't mind a little more pollution in a sky already the color of sardines. "Not a lot," he said. "Gooding was with the Road Commission off and on, mostly off, for only about five months before taking a medical." He told me which months. I took them down in my notebook.

"What sort of worker was he?"

"How good do you have to be to hold up a sign? Nothing remarkable on his work sheet; I guess he was reliable."

"Where'd he work?"

He started to read off street names, quadrant numbers, and dates from the printout sheet on his desk, then swore and slid it across to me. I wrote them down too, along with the foreman's name and home telephone number. "Anything else?"

"Nothing the computer noticed," he said.

"Okay, thanks." I got up, shook his hand, and went through the door, or almost. Blake and Fister were on their way in. The sergeant's fist was raised to rap on the door. When he saw me I pulled my head back out of range. He hesitated, then uncurled his fingers and smoothed down one side of his Fu Manchu. He said: "I should have guessed. The guy in Dearborn said someone was around asking about Gooding last night."

"Good morning, Sergeant," I said. "Officer."

"Let's clink him for interfering in a police investigation," suggested Fister. His long upper lip was skinned back to his gums, exposing teeth the shade of old plaster.

Blake ignored him. "You're screwing around with your license, Walker."

"Not technically, since I'm not working for anyone."

Fister said, "The law ain't in books, pal. It's here standing in front of you."

"Don't let us walk on your heels a second time," the sergeant said evenly. "We'll bend you till you break."

He walked around me into the office, followed a half-second later by his trained dog.

4

The foreman's name was Lawler. I tried his home number from a booth, got no answer, and called the county dispatcher's office, where a dead-voiced secretary informed me Lawler was due at a road construction site on Dequindre at two. That gave me three hours. I coaxed my heap up Woodward to the Detroit Public Library and spent the time in the microfilm room reading copies of the *News* and *Free Press* for the dates Gooding had worked flagging cars. No major robberies or hits had taken place in those vicinities at the time. So much for the theory that he had seen someone driving through whom he was better off not seeing. Rubbing floating type out of my eyes, I put a hamburger out of its misery at a lunch counter on Warren and took the Chrysler north to Dequindre. On the way I flipped on the radio in the middle of a news report on the bombing outside my office building. The announcer managed to get my name right, but that was about all.

A crew of eight were taking turns shoveling gravel and Elmer's Glue into a single pothole the size of a dimple at Remington. They would tip the stuff into the hole, pat it down, then walk half a block back to the truck for another load. Even then it didn't look as if they could make the job last until quitting time, but you never know. A hardhat crowding 50, with a great firm belly and sleeves rolled back past thick forearms burned to a dark cherry color, stood with one work shoe propped on the truck's rear bumper, eyes like twin slivers of blue glass watching the operation through the smoke of his cigarette. They didn't move as I pulled my car off to the side a safe distance from the county vehicle and got out. "Mr. Lawler?"

His only reaction was to reach up with a crusted forefinger and flick ash off his cigarette without removing it from between his lips. Since the gesture seemed more positive than negative, I gave him a look at my license photostat and told him what I was doing there. "Gooding ran interference for your crew," I wound up. "What can you tell me about him?"

"He knew which side of the sign said STOP and which said SLOW."

"Anything else?"

"Anything meaning what?" He still wasn't looking at me.

You run into him in every profession, the one bee in the hive who would rather sting than make honey. "Look," I said, "I'm just earning a living, like you and the lightning corps here. You look like someone who's talked to investigators; you know what I want. How did the old man get along with the other workers? Did you notice if there were any he was especially friendly with, or especially not friendly with? Did you overhear one of them saying something like, 'Gooding, I don't like you and I'm going to blow you up in your car'? Little things like that."

He flicked off some more ash. "I talked to investigators," he acknowledged. "Two years ago I seen a car run a stop sign on Jefferson and knock down a kid crossing the street. When I was getting set to testify against the driver his lawyer hired a detective to follow me around from bar to bar and prove in court I was a drunk and an unreliable witness. Yeah," he said, spitting out the butt, "I talked to investigators."

He walked away to look down into the pothole. I stood there for a moment, peeling cellophane off a fresh pack of Winstons. When he didn't return I put one in my mouth and went back to my car. A lanky black with a scar on his jaw and his hardhat balanced precariously on the back of his head climbed into the passenger's seat.

"I heard you talking to Lawler, mister." He talked through a sunny grin that brightened the interior. "He's not a bad dude; he's just had a run of bad luck."

"Must be tough." I touched a match to my weed and shook it out. Waiting.

"I knew Emmett Gooding some," he said.

I waited some more, looking at him. His grin was fixed. I got out my wallet and held up a ten-spot between the first and second fingers of my right hand. When he reached for it I pulled it back. He shrugged and sat back, still grinning. "Not enough to say much more than 'Hello' to," he went on. "There's like a wall around those old men, you know? Except to Jamie."

"Jamie?"

"James Dunrather, I think his right name was. White dude, about twenty-two. Long greasy blond hair and pimples. Lawler canned him a couple weeks back for selling dope on the job." He shook his head. "Ugly scene, man. He kept screaming about how he could get Lawler killed. Lawler just laughed."

I scraped some dust off the dash with the edge of the bill. "Dunrather and Gooding were friends?"

"Not friends. Jamie had a way of talking at you till you had to say something back just to get him to stop. I seen him talking at the old man that way on lunch break. Not the old man exclusive, mind you, just at anybody close. Gooding was the only one that didn't bother to get up and walk away."

"What'd he talk about?"

"Mostly he bragged about what a bad dude he was and all the bad dudes he knew. What you expect to hear from a part-time pusher. Then Gooding got sick and quit. But he come back."

"To work?"

He shook his head again. "He come to where we was tearing up pavement on Eight Mile. It was about a week before Jamie got canned. Man, Gooding looked about a hundred, leaning on them canes. He talked to Jamie for maybe ten minutes and then left in that beat-up Pontiac of his. Rest of us might've been in Mississippi for all the notice he took of us."

"You didn't hear what they were talking about?"

"Man, when that Rotomill starts ripping up asphalt —"

"Yeah," I said. "Where can I find this Dunrather?"

He shrugged, eyeing the sawbuck in my hand. I gave it to him. "Hope that's worth the job." I nodded through the windshield at Lawler, watching us from beside the pothole. My angel grinned with one foot on the pavement.

"Affirmative Action, man," he said. "It's a sweet country."

5

I made contact with Barry Stackpole at the *News,* who kept a personal file on street-level talent for his column. Jamie Dunrather had a record as long as Woodward Avenue for pushing pot and controlled substances, but no convictions, and an alias for each of his many addresses. Recent information had him living in a walkup over an adult bookstore on Watson. I promised Barry a dinner and tooled downtown.

There was a drunk snoring on the bottom step inside the street door with flies crawling on his face. I climbed over him and up a narrow squawking staircase with a gnawed rubber runner between mustard walls sprayed all over with words to live by. The upstairs hallway smelled of mold and thick paint that was fresh when Ford started paying five dollars a day. The building was as real as a stained Band-Aid on the floor of a YMCA pool. I rapped on Dunrather's door and flattened out against the wall next to the hinges, gripping the butt of my .38 in its belt clip. When no bullets splintered the panel I tried the knob. It gave.

Unclipping the gun, I pushed the door open slowly, going in with it to avoid being framed in the doorway. The shade was drawn over the room's only window, but enough light leaked in around it to fall on a ladderback chair mottled with old white paint, a dented table holding up a dirty china lamp and a portable TV, and a bed with a painted iron frame. The man dangling from the overhead fixture cast a gently drifting shadow as he twisted in the current of air stirring through the open door. He had a flexible wire like they hang pictures with sunk in the flesh of his neck, and his frog eyes and extended tongue were pale against his purple face. He was wearing faded jeans and track shoes and a red T-shirt with white letters that said MAKE ONLY BIG MISTAKES. You had to smile.

A floorboard sighed behind me while I was comparing the dead man's acned complexion and lank dishwater locks to my informant's description of Jamie Dunrather. I turned about a century too late. Later I thought I'd heard the swish, but all I was sure of was a bolt of white pain and a black mouth swallowing me.

6

"Put this where it hurts and shut up."

I'd expected gentler words on my way through the gates, but after staring for a moment at the wet handkerchief folded on the dusky pink palm I accepted it. I found the sticky lump behind my left ear with no trouble and fought back fresh darkness when the cold damp cloth touched the pulpy mass. Bitter bile climbed my throat. My thick tongue made me think of Dunrather and thought of Dunrather made the bile rise. I swallowed, vaguely conscious of having spoken.

"Did I say anything worth holding against me?"

Sergeant Blake ignored the question. He was sitting on the ladderback chair with his hands on his knees and his face too far from the floor where I was lying for me to make out. But I recognized the suit. Now I became aware of movement around me, and spotted the white coats from the morgue. They had freed the body and were wrapping it. Fister stood by watching.

"Bag his hands," Blake told them. To me: "I'm betting the wire made those cuts on his palms. He wouldn't grab it that tight unless he was trying to save his life. It wasn't suicide."

I said, "The guy who slugged me must've been hiding behind the door. He had to go past the drunk on the stairs on his way out. Maybe the drunk saw something."

"The drunk's at Headquarters now. But he was as gone as you, and the guy took the service stairs out back when he heard us coming. We found this on the steps." He tossed my wallet onto my chest. "It's been dusted. He wore gloves. If he didn't know who you were before, he knows now. Feed it to me."

I fed it to him, starting with what I'd learned at the road construction site. From past experience I didn't try to sit up. A pillow from the iron bed was under my head, which was full of bass fiddles tuning up.

"I say clink him," Fister put in. "It's his putzing around scared the killer into icing Dunrather."

"Unless Dunrather killed Gooding," I said.

Blake said, "No, it's good business not to clog up an investigation with too many killers. We got the same information you did by threatening to take Lawler downtown, and traced Dunrather through the computer. On our way up here we heard a street door slam on the other side of the building. Those new security places with no fire exits to speak of spoiled us; we didn't think to look for a back way."

I turned the handkerchief around to the cool side. "The bombing story hit the airwaves this afternoon. He's mopping up. Dunrather was a braggart, a poor risk."

"Everything about this case screams contract." The sergeant considered. "Except Gooding. There's no reason a pro would bother with an old man like that, and he couldn't have expected anyone but Gooding to blow up in Gooding's car."

I said, "He's too sloppy for a pro anyway. If a seasoned heavyweight wanted Dunrather's death to look like suicide he wouldn't have let him cut up his hands that way."

"Now that he knows who you are and how close you are,

whoever he is, I guess maybe we saved your butt by coming in when we did.''

"You never get a flat tire when you need one," Fister growled.

Blake leaned his forearms on his knees. "Cop killings are messy, Walker. Third parties tend to stop lead. It doesn't matter much to the guy who stops it whether it came from a Saturday Night Buster or a Police Special. Fister will type up your statement and we'll collect your signature later. You want a ride home?" He stood.

"My crate's parked around the corner," I said, sitting up slowly. The fiddles were louder in that position. "And your good cop, bad cop number's wasted on me."

"You're cluttering up the murder scene, Hot Wit." He held out my dented hat and gun, retrieved from the floor.

7

You can't live on the edge all the time, check behind all the doors and under all the beds and still be the sort of man who reads *Playboy*. But if you're lucky enough not to and live, it makes you alert enough next time to spot things like a cigarette end glowing like a single orange eye in the gloom behind your office window on your way to the front door of your building. I did, and forced my echoing skull to remember if I'd locked the inner sanctum. Then I decided remembering didn't matter, because people who don't mean you harm don't smoke in strange rooms while dusk is gathering without turning on a light.

I mounted the stairs like anyone else returning to his place of business just before closing, but slower than usual, thinking. You get a lot of thinking done in three flights. By the time I reached my floor I was pretty sure why Emmett Gooding had been marked for death, though I didn't know by whom, and none of it made sense anyway. It rarely does outside Nero Wolfe.

I walked right past the outer office door and through the one next to that, closing it behind me. My neighbor that week was a travel agent with one telephone and one desk and posters of places that looked nothing like Detroit on the walls. The agent's narrow sad brown face lit up when I entered, fell when he recognized me, and registered curiosity when I lifted his receiver and dialed Police Headquarters.

Sergeant Blake had just returned. When his voice finally came on the line I said, "How sure are you Emmett Gooding left no survivors?"

"Why?" Suspicion curled like smoke out of the earpiece.

"Because someone had to be named beneficiary on his life insurance policy."

"Who told you he had one?"

"You just did. Who is it?"

"I'm reading the report now. Twenty-five thousand goes to a girl out on the Coast, the daughter of an old friend who worked with Gooding on the line at Dearborn till he died nine years ago. But she hasn't left San Francisco this year."

"Double indemnity?" I pressed. "Fifty grand if he died by accident or mayhem?"

"Why ask me if you know? And how do you know?" I told him I was a detective. After a pause he said, "Anything else, or can I go home and introduce myself to my wife?"

"Do that. On the way you might stop by and pick up your cop-killer. He's waiting for me in my office."

The pause this time was longer. "Where are you?"

I told him.

"Okay, sit tight."

"What if he tries to leave?"

"Stop him." The line went dead.

I hung up and offered the travel agent a cigarette, but he

wasn't seeing the pack. He'd overheard everything. I lit one for myself and asked him if he'd sent anyone anywhere lately.

"Just my ex-wife and her boyfriend," he replied, coming out of it. "To Tahiti. On my alimony."

I grinned, but he could see my heart wasn't in it. The conversation flagged. I smoked and waited.

There had to be an insurance policy for Gooding to have done what he did. It had been done before, but the victims were always family men and any half-smart cop could wrap it up in an hour. Single men like my almost-client who had outlived whatever family or friends they'd had tended to throw off everyone but hunch-players like me and tireless pros like Blake who touched all the bases no matter how hopeless.

At two minutes past five I heard the door to my outer office close softly. Swearing quietly, I killed my butt in the travel agent's ashtray and advised him to climb under his desk. I didn't have to tell him twice. I moved out into the hallway with gun in hand.

His skinny back, clad in an army fatigue shirt, long black hair spilling to his shoulders, was just disappearing down the stairwell. I strode to the top of the stairs and cocked the .38. The noise made echoes. He started to turn. The overhead light painted a streak along the .45 automatic in his right hand.

"Uh-uh," I cautioned.

He froze in mid-turn. He wasn't much older than Dun-rather, with a droopy moustache that was mostly fuzz and a bulbous lower lip like a baby's. He was a third of the way down the flight.

"Junior button man," I sneered. "What'd Gooding pay you, a hundred?"

"Five hundred." His voice was as young as the rest of him. "He said it was all he had."

"He wasted it. He was a sick old man with nothing to look forward to but a nursing home. So like a lot of other sick old men he decided to go for the fast burn. But suicide would've voided his insurance and he wanted his dead friend's daughter to get something out of his death. The stroke made up his mind. He remembered Jamie Dunrather bragging about all the bad cats he knew, got your name from him, and paid you to take him out."

"I didn't want to get mixed up in no cop-killing," he said. "Who knew the old man was going to conk and someone else would eat that charge I stuck under his hood?"

"So when you heard about it you started covering your tracks. You cooled Dunrather and you would have cooled me too if the cops hadn't interrupted you." His thick lower lip dropped a millimeter. I pressed on. "You didn't know it was the cops, did you? You knew Gooding had been to see me, you thought he'd told me everything, and you figured that by waiting for me back here you could ambush me and be in the clear."

"Why not? When you didn't show by quitting time I decided to hit you at home. You was all I had to worry about, I thought."

"Pros give the cops more credit than that," I said. "But you'll never be a pro."

The air freshened in the stairwell, as if someone had opened the street door. I was talking to draw his attention from it. His knuckles whitened around the automatic's grip, and I saw he was wearing transparent rubber gloves.

"What'd he want to come see you for anyway?" he demanded.

"He changed his mind. When it came down to it he didn't really want to die. When he couldn't find you to call it off he was going to hire me to look for you. He read my name in the paper and that gave him the idea."

He made a thin keening sound between his teeth and twisted around the rest of the way, straightening his gun arm.

"Police! Drop it!"

A pro would have gone ahead and plugged me, then tended

to Blake on the second landing, but I was right about him. He swung back to fire down the stairs. Blake and I opened up at the same time. The reports of our .38s battered the walls. The man in the fatigue shirt dropped his .45 clattering down the steps, gripped the banister, and slid three feet before sliding off and piling into a heap of army surplus halfway down the flight.

In the echoing silence that followed, Officer Fister, who had entered the building a second behind his partner, bounded past Blake and bent to feel the man's neck for a pulse. He straightened after a moment. "He's killed his last cop."

"The hell with him," said the sergeant, holstering his gun under his left arm. Smoke curled spastically up the stairwell.

The dead man's name turned out to be Jarvis, and he had been questioned and released in connection with three unsolved homicides in the past year and a half. I didn't know him from Sam's cat. You can live in a city the size of Detroit a long time and never get to know all the killers if you're lucky.

Dead Soldier

1

NHA NELSON'S ORIENTAL FACE was shaped like an inverted raindrop, oval with a chin that came to a point. She just crested five feet and ninety pounds in a tight pink sweater and a black skirt that caught her legs just below the knees. Her eyes slanted down from a straight nose and her complexion was more beige than ivory. She was as Vietnamese as a punji stick.

I said, "My name's Amos Walker. I think we spoke on the telephone about a package I have for Mr. Nelson." I held up the bottle in the paper sack.

"Come in." She gave every consonant its full measure.

Carrying my wine like a partygoer, I followed her into a neat living room where two men sat watching television. One rose to grasp my hand. Reed Nelson was my height and age — just six feet and on the wrong side of 30 — but he had football shoulders under his checked shirt and wore his brass-colored hair cut very close. His brittle smile died short of his eyes. "My neighbor, Steve Minor."

I nodded to the other man, fortyish and balding, who grunted back but kept his seat. He was watching the Lions lose to Pittsburgh.

"Nha said a private detective called." Nelson's eyes went to the bottle. "It's about the tontine, isn't it?"

I said it was. He asked Steve Minor to excuse him, got a grunt in reply, and we adjourned to a paneled basement. Hunting prints covered the walls. Rifles and handguns occupied two glassed-in display cases, and a Browning automatic lay in pieces on a workbench stained with gun oil and crowded with cartridge-loading paraphernalia. My host cleared a stack of paper targets off one of a pair of crushed-leather armchairs and we sat down.

"Expecting someone?" I asked.

He smiled the halfway smile. "Friend of mine owns a range outside Dearborn. I was a sharpshooter in the army and I'd rather not lose the edge. If I were you I wouldn't smoke; you're sitting on a case of black powder."

I looked down at the edge of a carton stenciled EXPLOSIVE sticking out between the legs of my chair and put away my pack of Winstons.

"David Kurch hired me to find you and deliver the bottle," I said. "He's the lawyer you and the others left it with when you formed the tontine."

"I remember. He was an ARVN then, stationed in Que Noc." Nelson's expression turned in on itself. "That was only twelve years ago. It's hard to believe they're all dead."

"They are, though. Chuck Dundas stepped on a mine two feet shy of the DMZ in 'seventy. Albert Rule was MIA for seven years and has been declared dead. Fred Burlingame shot himself in New York last year, and Jerry Lynch died of cancer in August. Congratulations." I handed him the bottle.

He slid it out of the sack, fondled it. "It was bottled in some Frenchman's private vineyard in 'thirty-seven. Al found it in a ruined cellar near Hue, probably left behind when the French bugged out. The tontine was Fred's idea. The last man left was supposed to get the bottle. Were you over there?"

"Two years."

"Then you know how preoccupied we were with death. But, hell, I forgot all about this till you showed up. When I saw the package I remembered."

I passed him my receipt pad with a pen clipped to it. "If you'll sign this I'll shove off."

He read it swiftly and scribbled his name. "How'd you find me? I just moved to Detroit from Southfield, and my number's unlisted." He gave back the pad and pen.

"Kurch said you were an engineer at General Motors. I got it from Personnel."

"They have a hell of a nerve, after I just got fired."

"They cutting back again?"

He moved his head from side to side, but his eyes stayed on me. "They said I was a poor risk from a psychiatric stand-point."

"Are you?"

"You were in Nam. What do you think?"

I let that ride and got up. Crowd noise filtered down from the TV set upstairs. Someone had just made a touchdown. Nelson said, "You drink?"

I sat back down. "Do they make cars in Tokyo?"

This time his smile made it all the way. He turned his head and called, "Nha? Two glasses, please."

"What about your neighbor?" I asked.

"He'll understand. Steve and I aren't all that close. I only invite him over because I knew him slightly in Nam and he put me on to this house, not that that was such a favor with this mortgage staring at my throat. He introduced me to my wife."

On cue, Nha appeared, set a pair of stemmed glasses down on the workbench, and withdrew. She seemed flushed. Nelson scooped a Swiss Army knife out of a drawer in the bench and used the corkscrew to unstop the bottle. When the glasses were full of dark red liquid, he handed one over and raised his. "Chuck, Al, Fred, and Jerry. Four among the fifty thousand."

We sipped. It was good, but nothing beats twelve-year-old Scotch. "Were you married over there?"

He nodded. "She was working in a Saigon orphanage. Grew up there, after her parents got napalmed in 'sixty-five. You like being a private eye?"

We drank wine and sold each other our biographies. There

wasn't much to tell beyond the gaping hole of Vietnam. After an hour or so, the noise upstairs ceased abruptly. Steve Minor had switched off the set. Nelson replaced the cork in the bottle, which was now half empty. "There's another afternoon's drinking in here," he said, rising.

I was already on my feet. "Share it with your wife, or with someone else close."

"She's a teetotaler. And if there were anyone else close, do you think I'd be wasting it on a shamus I don't even know?" His eyes pleaded.

I said I'd call him. Upstairs, Nha saw me out without speaking. Minor had left.

2

It was three weeks before I made it back. I had spent much of that time following a city councilman's wife from male friend to male friend while her husband was on a junket to Palm Springs. Nelson greeted me at the door, explaining that Nha was out shopping. We killed the bottle in near-silence. He hadn't found a job and he wasn't talking much. It looked as if the novelty had worn off our relationship. We parted.

The rest of the month died painlessly. The Lions blew a late-season rally just before the playoffs. Snow was on the ground most other places. Detroit's streets were clogged with brown slush. Reed Nelson called me at the office on a Saturday and asked me to meet him somewhere for lunch.

"I've got a job interview in Houston next week," he said, when we were sharing a table in my favorite restaurant, one where the chef wore a shirt and didn't swat flies with his spatula. "Only the bank ate my last unemployment check and the savings account is down to double figures. When I applied for a loan, the manager of my friendly dependable finance company snickered and called in his assistant because he said he needed cheering up."

I blew on a spoonful of steaming chili. "What about old Steve? Army buddies are usually good for a few bucks."

"The hell with him."

I glanced up at Nelson's face. He'd lost weight. His cheeks were shadowed and there were purple thumbprints under his eyes. "How's Nha?" I asked.

"She's fine." The words cracked out like shots from a .22.

We ate. I said, "I'll give you two hundred for the Browning."

He hesitated. "It's not worth that. The trigger mechanism's sloppy and the barrel needs bluing."

"I always was a rotten businessman. We'll stop at my bank on the way back to the office. I'll come by later and pick up the automatic."

"Thanks, Amos. You ever need anything, just name it."

"Pass the salt."

3

I returned from a tail job early Monday afternoon. Whoever said travel is broadening never followed a possibly larcenous salesman clear to Toledo and sat up all night in a freezing car. I hadn't eaten since Sunday. Nursing the crick in my neck, I turned on the TV in my living room and lurched into the kitchen to find something to defrost. The volume was too high. When the sound came on, the name "Steven Minor" pasted me to the ceiling.

The picture was just blossoming on when I got back in. Floodlights illuminated two paramedics sliding a stretcher into the back of an ambulance. Then the camera cut to a male model in an overcoat standing in front of a house I recognized with a microphone in one hand. Police flashers throbbed sullenly in the street nearby.

"Police aren't saying yet what may have caused Nelson to shoot his neighbor and barricade himself in his house. But evidence suggests that the tragedy of Vietnam has just claimed another victim." The model identified himself and his grim face disappeared, to be replaced by a smiling one back at the Eyewitness News Desk. I left the set running and got out of there.

4

John Alderdyce was the lieutenant in charge of the investigation. He spoke to a big sergeant from the Tactical Mobile Unit, who reluctantly let me through the cordon. John's black and has been a friend since childhood, or as much of one as a plastic badge can hope to find among the blue brotherhood. "What's your billing in this?" he demanded when we were inside Nelson's house.

"Friend of the family." I scuffed a sole on a red stain on the carpet. It was still fresh, and it wasn't wine. The room was a shambles of overturned furniture and broken crockery. "When did Minor die?"

"He was DOA at Detroit Receiving." Alderdyce's face fluttered. "Damn it, who told you he's dead?"

"I'm a detective. Rumor has it you're with Homicide." I fed my face a butt. "What did I miss?"

"Right now it looks like this guy Nelson popped his cap, plugged his neighbor with a thirty-two auto, then locked himself in, holding his wife hostage. Hostage Negotiations people talked him into surrendering. He's wearing handcuffs in the basement. Vietnam vet, certified psycho, unemployed. They ought to print up a form report for this kind of thing with blanks where we can fill in the names, save on overtime."

"Any witnesses?"

"Don't need 'em. Nelson confessed. We're just waiting for the press to clear out so we can take him downtown and get it on tape. He and Minor were talking downstairs when he flipped. You ought to see that gun room. I guess you have." He nailed me. "Since when are you anybody's friend?"

"Even the garbageman rates a cup of coffee now and then. What's Nha say? That's his wife."

"I met her. Pretty. Did I ever tell you I had a crush on Nancy Kwan before I was married? She was hysterical when I got here. Nelson's wife, not Nancy. We called her doctor. He just left. She's in the bedroom, under sedation."

"I wonder how she got along without it when they burned her parents to death." I blew smoke. "Can I see Nelson?"

Alderdyce's eyes glittered in narrow slits. "As what? Friend or representative?"

I said friend. He considered, then nodded as if agreeing with himself and started for the stairs. I dogged his heels. Drops of blood mottled the steps. I halted.

"Where'd Minor get it?" I asked.

"In the right lung." The lieutenant looked back up at me from the bottom step. "He staggered up the stairs, bounced off some furniture on his way through the living room, and collapsed by the front door. Hospital says he drowned in his own blood. Anything wrong with that?"

"Are you asking as a friend or a policeman?"

He made a rude noise and resumed moving.

A cop in uniform and a plainclothesman I didn't know were guarding the prisoner, who was sitting in the chair I had occupied on my two visits, manacled wrists dangling between his knees. His shirt was soaked through with sweat. When I entered, he looked up and a tired smile tugged at the corners of his mouth. His features were cadaverous.

"I used your gun," he said. "Sorry."

"What's he mean, your gun?" snapped Alderdyce.

"Private joke," I said. "What happened, Reed?"

"They're saying I killed Steve. I was shooting at Charlie."

"Charlie?" Alderdyce's brow puckered.

"Viet Cong." I ditched my cigarette in an ashtray on the

workbench. "Shrinks call it Vietnam Flashback. Years after a vet leaves the jungle, something triggers his subconscious and he suddenly thinks he's back there surrounded by the enemy. He reacts accordingly."

"Oh yeah, that. As if murderers didn't have enough loopholes to squirt through as it was."

The telephone rang upstairs. Alderdyce jerked his head at the uniform, who went up to answer it.

"It's a legitimate dodge," I said. "Only not in this case, right, Reed? Steve Minor was the target all along."

The uniform's feet on the stairs were very loud in the silence that followed. "It's for you, Lieutenant," he said. "The lab."

Alderdyce pointed at me. "Hold that thought." He left us.

Five minutes later he returned. His eyes were very bright. "Blow your diminished capacity plea a kiss quick, Nelson. We're going Murder One."

5

"The D.A. won't buy it," said the plainclothesman, after a moment.

"Bet me. The lab found powder burns on Minor's shirt, but guess what? There weren't any around the wound. I called the hospital and checked."

"Proving?" I asked.

"Proving he wasn't wearing it when he was shot. Someone held it up and fired a bullet through it, then put it on him while he was dying upstairs to make us think otherwise. We know you were at Metro Airport an hour before the shooting, Nelson, and that the airline lost your reservation on a flight to Houston. Was Minor in bed with your wife when you came home, or did he just have time to take off his shirt?"

The prisoner leaped to his feet, but was shoved back into it by the other two officers. He opened his mouth, then closed it. Slouched.

"Neighbors reported only one shot, Lieutenant," the plain-clothesman pointed out. "And there was just one cartridge gone from the gun."

"They didn't hear the first because it was fired in the basement. And don't you think a man smart enough to know we'd question a chest wound without a corresponding hole in the shirt and then make up that psycho story to cover himself is smart enough to replace one of the spent shells? I want a crew here to search every inch of this house until they find where that second bullet went." He nailed me. "You knew Minor was the target. How? Did you know about him and Nelson's wife?"

"No, and I still don't," I said. "You're zero for two. Nelson never shot anyone. Not in this hemisphere, anyway."

Nelson glanced at me, then away. I continued before Alderdyce could ask any more questions.

"Reed was a sharpshooter over there. Still is; he told me he keeps in practice. There's no way, if he thought Minor was a Viet Cong, that he'd miss the heart at this range and give Charlie a chance to retaliate. And if it was Minor he wanted to kill, he would've made sure his victim didn't hang around long enough to talk. It's my guess he was shot before Reed got here."

"No! I killed him!" This time the cops held the prisoner in his chair.

"His car was parked in the driveway when the neighbors heard the gun go off," Alderdyce snarled. The skin on his face was drawn so tight it shone blue, as it often did when I was speaking.

"You said yourself it was the second shot they heard," I reminded him. "That one was his, to keep anyone from wondering why Minor didn't have his shirt on in his neighbor's house, and he did it upstairs because he knew it wasn't safe to pull a trigger in the basement with so much black powder lying around. Just one other person could have fired the fatal bullet. Just one other person was in the house at the time." I breathed some air. "What were Nha and Steve Minor to each other back in Vietnam, Reed?"

"Prostitute and pimp."

Alderdyce and I turned. Nha Nelson, barefoot in a Chinese house dress, her hair down and disheveled, was leaning against the wall at the bottom of the stairwell. Her face was streaked and puffy.

"Don't, Nha," pleaded her husband.

"I should not have let it come this far." She spoke slowly, like a record winding down. The doctor's sedative had furred the fine edge. "Minor made money on the side running prostitutes in Saigon. I was one of six. When his tour ended, he introduced us all to GIs he knew, hoping some of us would marry and he could blackmail the husbands later by threatening to tell all their friends and business associates what their wives used to do for a living.

"Reed was an engineer for a large corporation, the perfect victim. But he lost his job before Minor could begin squeezing him. Then he blackmailed me, but not for money. He was a depraved man. He said if I did not have sex with him he would tell Reed I lied about my past. I agreed."

Her eyes filled and ran over. Nelson said her name. She acted as if she hadn't heard. "I love my husband. I was afraid he would leave me if he knew the truth. Minor waited until Reed left for the airport and then he came over to collect. But I could not do it. I had done it many times, with many men, but that was in Vietnam, before I had Reed. I excused myself while Minor was undressing and came down here for a gun. I wanted only to scare him, to make him leave. He suspected something and followed me. When I heard him on the stairs I panicked. I turned and —" Bitter tears strangled her.

I gave her my handkerchief. She wiped her eyes and nose. Nelson was weeping too, his face buried in his hands, the chain dangling between the wrists. Quiet rolled in and sat down. Alderdyce booted it out. "Do you have the names of the other five women?"

"Three of them," she said. "The other two didn't marry the men Minor wanted them to. I even know the husbands' names and what cities they lived in. He bragged to me about how he had traveled around the country all this time, setting up shop wherever a victim was. That's what he called it, 'setting up shop.' "

The uniform took her elbow gently and steered her around as if she were a sleepy child. Nelson stood.

"Thanks for nothing, Walker."

I said, "I'll be surprised if the D.A. presses charges. If he does he'll lose."

"So what? I'm going to end up in the nut ward sooner or later. My way it counted for something. Why'd you have to take that away from me? We were friends for a while."

I had nothing to throw at that. The plainclothesman prodded him forward and up the steps.

Alderdyce hung back. He had spotted the empty wine bottle, standing in a back corner of the workbench behind a can of gun stock refinisher. "That looks out of place here. Maybe I should have it dusted."

"Forget it." I picked it up and chucked it into the wastebasket. "Dead soldier."

Eight Mile
and Dequindre

THE CLIENT was a no-show, as four out of ten of them tend to be.

She had called me in the customary white heat, a woman with one of those voices you hear in supermarkets and then thank God you're not married, and arranged to meet me someplace not my office and not her home. The bastard had been paying her the same alimony for the past five years, she'd said, and she wanted a handle on his secret bank accounts to prove he was making twice as much as when they split. In the meantime she'd cooled down or the situation had changed or she'd found a private investigator who worked even cheaper than I did, leaving me to drink yellow coffee alone at a linoleum counter in a gray cinderblock building on Dequindre at Eight Mile Road. I was just as happy. Why I'd agreed to meet her at all had to do with a bank balance smaller than my IQ, and since talking to her I'd changed my mind and decided to refer her to another agency anyway. So I worked on my coffee and once again considered taking on a security job until things got better.

A portable radio behind the counter was tuned to a Pistons game, but the guy who'd poured my coffee, lean and young with butch-cut red hair and a white apron, didn't look to be listening to it, whistling while he chalked new prices on the blackboard menu on the wall next to the cash register. Well, it was March and the Pistons were where they usually were in the standings at that time and nobody in Detroit was listening. I asked him what the chicken on a roll was like.

"Better than across the street," he said, wiping chalk off his hands onto the apron.

Across the street was a Shell station. I ordered the chicken anyway; unless he skipped some lines it was too far down on the board for him to raise the price before I'd eaten it. He opened a stainless steel door over the sink and took the plastic off a breaded patty the color of fresh sawdust and slapped it hissing on the griddle.

We'd had the place to ourselves for a while, but then the pneumatic front door whooshed and sucked in a male customer in his thirties and a sportcoat you could hear across the street, who cocked a hip onto a stool at the far end of the counter and asked for a glass of water.

"Anything to go with that?" asked Butch, setting an amber-tinted tumbler in front of him.

"No, I'm waiting for someone."

"Coffee, maybe."

"No, I want to keep my breath fresh."

"Oh. That kind of someone." He wiped his hands again. "It's okay for now, but if the place starts to fill up you'll have to order something, a Coke or something. You don't have to drink it."

"Sounds fair."

"This ain't a bus station."

"I can see that."

Nodding, Butch turned away and picked up a spatula and flipped the chicken patty and broke a roll out of plastic. The guy in the sportcoat asked how the game was going, but Butch either didn't hear him or didn't want to. The guy gave up on him and glanced down the counter at me.

"You waiting for someone too?"

"I was," I said. "Now I'm waiting for that bird."

"Stood you up, huh? That's tough."

"I'm used to it."

He hesitated, then got down and picked up his glass and carried it to my end and climbed onto the stool next to mine. Up close he was about 30, freckled, with a double chin starting and dishwater hair going thin in front. A triangle of white shirt showed between his belt buckle and the one button he had fastened on the jacket. He had prominent front teeth and looked a little like Howdy Doody. "This girl I'm waiting for would never stand anyone up," he said. "She's got manners."

"Yeah?"

"No, really. Looks too. Here's her picture." He took a fat curved wallet out of his hip pocket and showed me the head and torso of a blonde in a red bandana top, winking and grinning at the camera. She stank professional model.

"Nice," I said. "What's she do?"

"Waitress at the Peacock's Roost. That'll change when we're married. I don't want my wife to work."

"The girls in steel-rimmed glasses and iron pants will burn their bras on your lawn."

"To hell with them. Rena won't have anything to do with that kind. That's her name, Rena."

"I think it's dead now," I told Butch.

He landed the chicken patty on one half of the roll and planted the other half on top and put it on a china saucer and set the works on the linoleum. Howdy Doody finished putting away his wallet and stuck his right hand across his body in front of me. "Dave Tillet."

"Amos Walker." I shook the hand and picked up the sandwich. As it turned out I couldn't have done any worse across the street at the Shell station.

Tillet sipped his water. "That clock right?"

Butch looked up to see which clock he meant. There was only one in the place, advertising Stroh's beer on the wall behind the counter. "Give or take a minute."

"She ought to be here now. She's usually early."

"Maybe she stood you up after all," I said.

"Not Rena."

I ate the chicken and Tillet drank his water and the guy behind the counter picked up his chalk and resumed changing prices and didn't listen to the basketball game. I wiped my mouth with a cheesy paper napkin and asked Butch what the tariff was. He said "Buck ninety-five." I got out my wallet.

"Maybe I better call her," said Tillet. "That phone working?"

Butch said it was. Tillet drained his glass and went to the pay telephone on the wall just inside the door. I paid for the sandwich and coffee. "Well, good luck," I told Tillet on my way past him.

"What? Yeah, thanks. You too." He was listening to the purring in the earpiece. I pushed on the glass door.

Two guys were on their way in and I stepped aside and held the door for them. They were wearing dark Windbreakers and colorful knit caps and when they saw me they reached up with one hand apiece and rolled the caps down over their faces and the caps turned into ski masks. Their other hands were coming out of the slash pockets of the Windbreakers and when I saw that I jumped back and let go of the door, but the man closest to it caught it with his arm and stuck a long-barreled .22 target pistol in my face while his partner came in past him and lamped the place quickly and then put the .22's twin almost against Tillet's noisy sportcoat. Three flat reports slapped the air. Tillet's mouth was open and he was leaning one shoulder against the wall and he hadn't had time to start falling or even know he was shot when the guy fired again into his face and then deliberately moved the gun and gave him another in the ear. The guy's buddy wasn't watching. He was looking at me through the eyeholes in his mask and his eyes were as flat and gray as nickels on a pad. They held no more expression than the empty blue hole also staring me in the face.

Then the pair left, Gray Eyes backing away with his gun still on me while his partner walked swiftly to a brown Plymouth Volare and around to the driver's side and got in and then

Gray Eyes let himself in the passenger's side and they were rolling before he got the door closed.

Tillet fell then, crumpling in on himself like a gas bag deflating, and folded to the floor with no more noise than laundry makes skidding down a chute. Very bright red blood leaked out of his ear and slid into a puddle on the gray linoleum floor.

I ran out to the sidewalk in time to see the Plymouth take the corner. Forget about the license number. I wasn't wearing a gun. I hardly ever needed one to meet a woman in a diner.

When I went back in, the counterman was standing over Tillet's body, wiping his hands over and over on his apron. His face was as pale as the cloth. The telephone receiver swung from its cord and the metallic purring on the other end was loud in the silence following the shots. I bent and placed two fingers on Tillet's neck. Nothing was happening in the big artery. I straightened, picked up the receiver, worked the plunger, and dialed 911. Standing there waiting for someone to answer I was sorry I'd eaten the chicken.

2

They sent an Adam and Eve team, a white man and a black woman in uniform. You had to look twice at the woman to know she was a woman. They hadn't gotten around to cutting uniforms to fit them, and her tunic hung on her like a tarpaulin. Her partner had baby fat in his cheeks and a puppy moustache. His face went stiff when he saw the body. The woman might have been looking at a loose tile on the floor for all her expression gave up. Just to kill time I gave them the story, knowing I'd have to do it all over again for the plainclothes team. Butch was sitting on one of the customers' stools with his hands in his lap and whenever they looked at him he nodded in agreement with my details. The woman took it all down in shorthand.

The first string arrived ten minutes later. Among them was a black lieutenant, coarse-featured and heavy in the chest and shoulders, wearing a gray suit cut in heaven and a black tie with a silver diamond pattern. When he saw me he groaned.

"Hello, John," I said. "This is a hike north from Head-quarters."

John Alderdyce of Detroit Homicide patted all his pockets and came up with an empty Lucky Strikes package. I gave him a Winston from my pack and took one for myself and lit them both. He squirted smoke and said, "I was eight blocks from here when I got the squeal. If I'd known you were back of it I'd have kept driving."

John and I had known each other a long time, a thing I admitted to a lot more often than he did. While I was recounting the last few minutes in the life of Dave Tillet, a police photographer came in and took pictures of the body from forty different angles and then a bearded black Homicide sergeant I didn't know tugged on a pair of surgical gloves and knelt and started going through Tillet's clothes. Butch had recovered from his shock by this time and came over to watch. "Them gloves are to protect the fingerprints, right?" he asked.

"Wrong. Catch." The sergeant tossed him Tillet's wallet.

Butch caught it against his chest. "It's wet."

"That's why the gloves."

Butch thought about it, then dropped the wallet quickly and mopped his hands on his apron.

"Can the crap," barked Alderdyce. "What's inside?"

Still chuckling, the sergeant picked up the wallet and went through the contents. He whistled. "Christ, it's full of C-notes. Eight, ten, twelve — this guy was carrying fifteen hundred bucks on his hip."

"What else?"

The celluloid windows gave up a Social Security card and a

temporary driver's license, both made out to David Edward Tillet, and the picture of the blonde.

"That Rena?" Alderdyce asked.

I nodded. "She waits tables at the Peacock's Roost, Tillet said."

Alderdyce told the sergeant to bag the wallet and its contents. To me: "You saw these guys before they pulled down their ski masks?"

"Not enough before. They were just guys' faces. I didn't much look at them till they went for the guns. The trigger was my height, maybe ten pounds to the good. His partner gave up a couple of inches, same build, gray eyes." I described the getaway car.

"Stolen," guessed the sergeant. He stood and slid a glassine bag containing the wallet into the side pocket of his coat.

Alderdyce nodded. "It was a market job. The girl was the finger. She's smoke by now. Dope?"

"That or numbers," said the sergeant. "He's a little pale for either one in this town, but the rackets are nothing if not an equal opportunity employer. Nobody straight carries cash any more."

"I still owe a thousand on this building." Butch's upper lip was folded over his chin. "I guess I'd be dumb to pay it off now."

"The place is made," the sergeant told him.

"Yeah?" The counterman looked hopefully at Alderdyce, who grunted.

"The Machus Red Fox is booked into next year and has been ever since Hoffa caught his last ride from in front of it."

"Yeah?"

The lieutenant was still looking at me. "When can you come down and sign a statement?"

"Whenever it's ready. I'm not exactly swamped."

"Five o'clock, then." He paused. "Your part in this is finished, right?"

"When I work I get paid," I said.

"How come that doesn't comfort me?"

I said I'd see him at five.

The morgue wagon was just creaking its brakes in front when I came out into the afternoon sunlight and walked around the blue-and-white and a couple of unmarked units and a green Fiat to my heap. I was about to get in behind the wheel when I stopped and looked again at the Fiat. The girl Dave Tillet had called Rena was sitting in the driver's seat, staring at the blank cinderblock wall in front of the windshield.

3

I opened the door on the passenger side and got in next to her. She jumped in the seat and looked at me quickly. Her honey-colored hair was caught in a clasp behind her neck, below which a kind of ponytail hung down her back, and she was wearing a tailored navy suit over a cream-colored blouse open at the neck and jet buttons in her ears, but I recognized her large smoky eyes and the just slightly too-wide mouth that was built for grinning, although she wasn't grinning. The interior of the little car smelled of car and sandalwood.

She snatched up a blue bag from the seat and her hand vanished inside. I caught her wrist. She struggled, but I applied pressure and her face went white and she stopped struggling. I relaxed the hold, but just a little.

"Dave's dead," I said. "You can't help him now."

She said nothing. On "dead," her head jerked as if I'd smacked her. I went on.

"You don't want to be here when the cops come out. They've got your picture and they think you fingered Dave."

"That's stupid." Her voice came from just in back of her tongue. I didn't know how it was normally.

"It's not stupid. He was expecting you and got five slugs from a twenty-two. The cops know where you work and pretty soon they'll know where you live and when they find you they'll book you as a material witness and change it to accessory to the fact later."

"You talk like you're not one of them."

"Get real, lady. If I were we wouldn't be sitting here talking. On the other hand, if you set up Dave deliberately you wouldn't be here at all. It could just be you're someone who could use some help."

Her lips twisted. "And it could just be you're someone who could give it."

"We're talking," I reminded her. "I'm not hollering cop."

"Who the hell are you?"

I told her. Her lips twisted some more.

"A cheap snooper. I should have guessed it would be something like that."

I said, "It's a buyer's market. I don't set the price."

"What's the price?"

"Some truth. Not right now, though. Not here. Let's go somewhere."

"You go," she said. "I've got a pistol in this purse and when I pull the trigger it won't much matter whether it's inside or outside."

I didn't move. "Guns, everybody's got 'em. After a killer's screwed one in your face the rest aren't so scary."

We sat like that for a while, she with her hand in the purse and turned a little in the seat so that one silken knee showed under the hem of her pleated skirt while a cramp crawled across the palm I had clenched on her wrist. The morgue crew came out the front door of the diner wheeling a stretcher with a zipped bag full of Dave Tillet on it and folded the works into the back of the wagon. Rena didn't look at them. Finally I let go of her and got out one of my cards and a pen. I moved slowly to avoid attracting bullets.

"I'll just put my home address and telephone number on the back," I said, writing. "Open twenty-four hours. Just ring and ask for Amos. But do it before the cops get you or I'm just another spent shell."

She said nothing. I tucked the card under the mirror she had clamped to the sun visor on the passenger side and got out and into my crate and started the motor and swung out into the street and took off with my cape flying behind me.

4

I made some calls from the office, but none of the security firms or larger investigation agencies in town had anything to farm out. I bought myself a drink from the file drawer in the desk and when that was finished I bought myself another, and by then it was time to go to Police Headquarters at 1300 Beaubien, or just plain 1300 as it's known in town. The lady detective who announced me to John Alderdyce was too much detective not to notice the Scotch on my breath but too much lady to mention it. Little by little they are changing things down there, but it's a slow process.

In John's office I gave my story again to a stenographer while Alderdyce and the bearded sergeant listened for variations. When the steno left to type up my statement I asked John what he'd found out.

"Tillet kept the books for Great Lakes Importers. Ever hear of it?"

"Front for the Mob."

"So you say. It's worth a slander suit if you say it in public, they're that well screened with lawyers and holding corporations." He broke open a fresh pack of Luckies and fired one up with a Zippo. I already had a Winston going. "Tillet rented a house in Southfield. A grand a month."

"Any grand jury investigations in progress?" I asked. "They're hard on the bookkeeping population."

He shook his head. "We got a call in to the feds, but even if they get back to us we'll still have to go up to the mountain to get any information out of those tight-mouthed clones. We're pinning our hopes on the street trade and this woman Rena. Especially her."

"What'd you turn on her?"

"She works at the Peacock's Roost like you said, goes by Rena Murrow. She didn't show up for the four P.M. shift today. She's got an apartment on Michigan and we have men waiting for her there, but she's empty tracks by now. Tillet's landlady says he's been away someplace on vacation. Lying low. Whoever wanted him out in the open got to Rena. By all accounts she is a woman plenty of scared accountants would break cover to meet."

"Maybe someone used her."

He grinned that tight grin that was always bad news for someone. "Your license to hunt Dulcineas still valid?"

"Everyone needs a hobby," I said. "Stamps are sissy."

"Safer, though. According to the computer, this damsel has two priors for soliciting, but that was before she started bumming around with one Peter Venito. 'Known former associate,' it says in the printout. Computers have no romance in their circuits."

I smoked and thought. Peter Venito, born Pietro, had come up through the Licavoli mob during Prohibition and during the old Kefauver Committee hearings had been identified as one of the five dons on the board of governors of that fraternal organization the Italian Anti-Defamation League would have us believe no longer exists.

"Venito's been dead four or five years," I said.

"Six. But his son Paul's still around and a slice off the old pizza. His secretary at Great Lakes Importers says he's in Las Vegas. Importing."

"Anything on the street soldiers?"

"Computer got a hernia sorting through gray eyes and the heights and builds you gave us. I'd go to the mugs but you say you didn't get a long enough hinge at them without their masks, so why go into golden time? Just sign the statement and give my eyes a rest from your ugly pan."

The stenographer had just returned with three neatly typewritten sheets. I read my words and wrote my name at the bottom. "I have it on good authority I'm a heartbreaker," I told Alderdyce, handing him the sheets.

"What's a Dulcinea, anyway?" asked the sergeant.

5

The shooting at Eight Mile and Dequindre was on the radio. They got my name and occupation right, anyway. I switched to a music station and drove through coagulating dusk to my little three-room house west of Hamtramck, where I put my key in a door that was already unlocked. I'd locked it when I left that morning.

I went back for the Luger I keep in a special compartment under the dash, and when I had a round in the chamber I sneaked up on the door with my back to the wall and twisted the knob and pushed the door open at arm's length. When no bullets tore through the opening I eased the gun and my face past the door frame. Rena was sitting in my one easy chair in the living room with a .32 Remington automatic in her right hand and a bottle of Scotch and a half-full glass standing on the end table on the other side.

"I thought it might be you," she said. "That's why I didn't shoot."

"Thanks for the vote of confidence."

"You ought to get yourself a dead-bolt lock. I've known how to slip latches since high school."

"All they taught me was algebra." I waved the Luger. "Can we put up the artillery? It's starting to get silly."

She laid the pistol in her lap. I snicked the safety into place on mine and put it on the table near the door and closed the door behind me. She picked up her glass and sipped from it.

"You buy good whisky. Keyhole-peeping must pay pretty good."

"That's my Christmas bottle."

"Your friends must like you."

"I bought it for myself." I went into the kitchen and got a glass and filled it from the bottle.

She said, "The cops were waiting for me at my place. One of them was smoking a pipe. I smelled it the minute I hit my floor."

"The world's full of morons. Cops come in for their share." I drank.

"What's it going to cost me to get clear of this?"

"How much you got?"

She glanced down at the blue bag wedged between her left hip and the arm of the chair. It was a nice hip, long and slim with the pleated navy skirt stretched taut over it. "Five hundred."

I shrugged.

"All of it?"

"It'd run you that and more to put breathing space between you and Detroit," I said. "It wouldn't buy you a day in any of the safe houses in town."

"What will I eat on?"

"On the rest of it. You knew damn well I'd set my price at whatever you said you had, so I figure you knocked it down by at least half."

She twisted her lips in that way she had and opened the bag and peeled three C-notes and four fifties off a roll that would choke a tuba. I accepted the bills and riffled through them and stuck the wad in my inside breast pocket.

"How's Paul?" I asked.

"He's in Vegas," she answered automatically. Then she looked up at me quickly and pursed her lips. I cut her off.

"The cops know about you and old Peter Venito, may he rest in peace. The word on the street is young Paul inherited everything."

"Not everything."

I was lighting a cigarette and so didn't bother to shrug. I flipped the match into an ashtray. "Dave Tillet."

"I liked Dave. He wasn't like the others that worked for Paul. He wanted to get out. He was all set to take the CPA exam in May."

"He didn't just like you," I said. "He was planning to marry you."

She raised her eyebrows. They were darker than her hair, two inverted commas over eyes that I saw now were ringed with red under her make-up. "I didn't know," she said quietly.

"Who dropped the dime on him?"

Now her face took on the hard sheen of polished metal. "All right, so you tricked me into admitting I knew Paul Venito. That doesn't mean I know the heavyweights he hires."

"You've answered my question. When a bookkeeper for the Mob starts making leaving noises, his employers start wondering where he's going with what he knows. What'd Venito do to get you to set up Dave?"

"I didn't set him up!"

I smoked and waited. In the silence she looked at the wall behind me and then at the floor and then at her hands on the purse in her lap and then she drained her glass and refilled it. The neck of the bottle jingled against the rim. She drank.

"Dave went into hiding a week ago because of some threats he said he got over his decision to quit," she said. "None of them came from Paul, but from his own fellow workers. He gave me a number where he could be reached and told me to memorize it and not write it down or give it to anyone else. I'd gone with Paul for a while after old Peter died and Paul knew I was seeing Dave and he came to my apartment yesterday and asked me where he could reach Dave. I wouldn't give him the number. He said he just wanted to talk to him and would I arrange a meeting without saying it would be with Paul. He was afraid Dave's fellow workers had poisoned him against the whole operation. He wanted to make Dave a cash offer to keep quiet about his, Paul's, activities and that if I cared for him and his future I'd agree to help. I said okay. It sounded like the Paul Venito I used to know," she added quickly. "He would spend thousands to avoid hurting someone; he said that was bad business and cost more in the long run."

"Who picked the spot?"

"Paul did. He called it neutral territory, halfway between Dave's place in Southfield and Paul's office downtown."

"It's also handy to expressways out of the city," I said. "So you set up the parley. Then what?"

"I called Paul's office today to ask him if I could sit in on the meeting. His secretary told me he left for Las Vegas last night. That's when I knew he had no intention of keeping his appointment, or of being anywhere near the place when whoever was keeping it for him went in to see Dave. I broke every law driving here, but —"

The metal sheen cracked apart then. She said "Damn" and dug in her purse for a handkerchief. I watched her pawing blindly through the contents for a moment, then handed her mine. If it was an act it was sweet.

"Did anyone follow you here?" I asked.

She wiped her eyes, blew her nose as discreetly as a thing like that can be done, and looked up. Her cheeks were smeared blue-black. That was when I decided to believe her. You don't look like her and know how to turn the waterworks on and off without knowing how to keep your mascara from running too.

"I don't think so," she said. "I kept an eye out for cops and parked around the corner. Why?"

"Because if what you told me is straight, you're next on Venito's list of Things To Do Today. You're the only one who can connect him to that diner. Have you got a place to stay?"

"I guess one of the girls from the Roost could put me up."

"No, the cops will check them out. They'll hit all the hotels and motels too. You'd better stay here."

"Oh." She gave me her crooked smile. "That plus the five hundred, is that how it goes?"

"I'll toss you for the bed. Loser gets the couch."

"You don't like blondes?"

"I'm not sure I ever met one. But it has something to do with not going to the bathroom where you eat. Give me your keys and I'll stash your car in the garage. Cops'll have a BOL out on it by now."

She was reaching inside her purse when the door buzzer blew us a raspberry. Her hand went to the baby Remington. I touched a finger to my lips and pointed at the bedroom door. She got up clutching her purse and the gun and went into the bedroom and pushed the door shut, or almost. She left a crack. I retrieved my handkerchief stained with her make-up from the chair and put it in a pocket and picked up the Luger and said, "Who is it?"

"Alderdyce."

I opened the door. He glanced down at the gun as if it were a loose button on my jacket and walked around me into the living room. "Expecting trouble?"

"It's a way of life in this town." I safetied the Luger and returned it to the table.

"You alone?" He looked around.

"Who's asking, you or the department?"

He said nothing, circling the living room with his hands in his pockets. He stopped near the bedroom door and sniffed the air. "Nice cologne. A little feminine."

"Even detectives have a social life," I said.

"You couldn't prove it by me."

I killed my cigarette butt and fought the tug to reach for a replacement. "You didn't come all this way to do Who's On First with me."

"We tracked down Paul Venito. I thought you'd want to know."

"In Vegas?"

He moved his large close-cropped head from side to side slowly. "At Detroit Metropolitan Airport. Stiff as a stick in the trunk of a stolen Oldsmobile."

6

The antique clock my grandfather bought for his mother knocked out the better part of a minute with no competition. I shook out my last Winston and smoothed it between my fingers. "Shot?"

"Three times with a twenty-two. Twice in the chest, once in the ear. Sound familiar?"

"Yeah." I speared my lips with the cigarette and lit up. "How long's he been dead?"

"That's up to the M.E. Twelve hours anyway. He was a cold cut long before Tillet bought it."

"Which means what?"

He shook his head again. His coarse face was drawn in the light of the one lamp I had burning.

"My day rate's two-fifty," I said. "If you're talking about consulting."

"I'm talking about withholding evidence and obstruction of justice. The Murrow woman is getting to be important, and I think you know where she is."

I smoked and said nothing.

"It's this tingly feeling I get," he said. "Happens every time a case involves a woman and Amos Walker too."

"Christ, John, all I did was order the chicken on a roll."

"I hope that's all you did. I sure hope."

We watched each other. Suddenly he seized the knob and pushed open the bedroom door, scooping his Police Special out of his belt holster. I lunged forward, then held back. The room was empty.

He went inside and looked out the open window and checked the closet and got down in pushup position to peer under the bed. Rising, he holstered the .38 and dusted his palms off against each other. "Perfume's stronger in here," he observed.

"I told you I was a heartbreaker."

"Make sure that's all you're breaking."

"Is this where you threaten to trash my license?"

"That's up to the state police," he said. "What I can do is tank you and link your name to that diner shoot for the reporters until little old ladies in Grosse Pointe won't trust you to walk their poodles."

On that chord he left me. John and I had been friendly a long time. But no matter how long you are something, you are not that something a lot longer.

7

So far I had two corpses and no Rena Murrow. It was time to punt. I dialed Great Lakes Importers, Paul Venito's legitimate front, but there was no answer. Well, it was way past closing time; in an orderly society even the crooks keep regular hours. I thawed something out for supper and watched an old Kirk Douglas film on television and turned in.

The next morning was misty gray with the bitter-metal smell of rain in the air. I broke out the foul-weather gear and drove to the Great Lakes building on East Grand River.

The reception area, kept behind glass like expensive cigars in a tobacco shop, was oval-shaped with passages spiking out from it, decorated in orange sherbet with a porcelain doll seated behind a curved desk. She wore a tight pink cashmere sweater and a black skirt slit to her ears.

"Amos Walker to see Mr. Venito," I said.

"I'm sorry. Mr. Venito's suffered a tragic accident." Her voice was honey over velvet. It would be.

"Who took his place?"

"That would be Mr. DeMarco. But he's very busy."

"I'll wait." I pulled a Thermos bottle full of hot coffee out of the slash pocket of my trenchcoat and sat down on an orange couch across from her desk.

The porcelain doll lifted her telephone receiver and spoke into it. A few minutes later, two men in tailored blue suits came out of one of the passages and stood over me, and that was when the front crumbled.

"Position."

I wasn't sure which of them had spoken. They looked alike down to the scar tissue over their eyes. I screwed the top back on the Thermos and stood and placed my palms against the wall. One of them kicked my feet apart and patted me down from tie to socks, removing my hat last and peering inside for atomic devices. I wasn't carrying. He replaced the hat.

"Okay, this way."

I accompanied them down the passage with a man on either side. We went through a door marked P. VENITO into an office the size of Hart Plaza with green wall-to-wall carpeting and one wall that was all glass, before which stood a tall man with a fringe of gray hair and a neat Vandyke beard. His suit was tan and clung like sunlight to his trim frame.

"Mr. Walker?" he said pleasantly. "I'm Fred DeMarco. I was Mr. Venito's associate. This is a terrible thing that's happened."

"More terrible for him than you," I said.

He cocked his head and frowned. "This office, you mean. It's just a room. Paul's father had it before him and someone will have it after me. I recognized your name from the news. Weren't you involved in the shooting of this Tillet person yesterday?"

I nodded. "If you call being a witness involved. But you don't have to call him 'this Tillet person.' He worked for you."

"He worked for Great Lakes Importers, like me. I never knew him. The firm employs many people, most of whom I haven't had the chance to meet."

"My information is he was killed because he was leaving Great Lakes and someone was afraid he'd peddle what he knew."

"We're a legitimate enterprise, Mr. Walker. We have nothing to hide. Tillet was let go. Our accounting department is handled mostly by computers now and he elected not to undergo retraining. Whatever he was involved with outside the firm that led to his death has nothing to do with Great Lakes."

"For someone who never met him you know a lot about Tillet," I said.

"I had his file pulled for the police."

"Isn't it kind of a big coincidence that your president and one of your bookkeepers should both be shot to death within a few hours of each other, and with the same caliber pistol?"

"The police were here again last night to ask that same question," DeMarco said. "My answer is the same. If, like Tillet, Paul had dangerous outside interests, they are hardly of concern here."

I got out a Winston and tapped it on the back of my hand. "You've been on the laundering end too long, Mr. DeMarco. You think you've gotten away from playing hardball. Just because you can afford a tailor and a better barber doesn't mean you aren't still Freddy the Mark, who came up busting heads for Peter Venito in the bad old days."

One of the blue suits backhanded the cigarette out of my mouth as I was getting set to light it. "Mr. DeMarco doesn't allow smoking."

"That's enough, Andy." DeMarco's tone was even. "I was just a boy when Prohibition ended, Walker. Peter took me in and almost adopted me. I learned the business and when I got back from the war and college I showed him how to modernize, cut expenses, and increase profits. For thirty years I practically ran the organization. Then Peter died and his son took over and I was back to running errands. But for the good of the firm I drew my pay and kept my mouth shut. We're legitimate now and I mean for it to stay that way. I wouldn't jeopardize it for the likes of Dave Tillet."

"I think you would do just that. You remember a time when

no one quit the organization, and when Tillet gave notice and you found out young Paul had arranged to buy his silence instead of making dead sure of it, you took Paul out of the way and then slammed the door on Tillet."

"You're fishing, Walker."

"Why not? I've got Rena Murrow for bait."

The room got quiet. Outside the glass, fourteen floors down, traffic glided along Grand River with all the noise of fish swimming in an aquarium.

"She set up the meet with Tillet for Venito," I went on. "She can tie Paul to that diner at Eight Mile and Dequindre and with a little work the cops will tie you to that trunk at Metro Airport. She can finger your two button men. Looking down the wrong end of life in Jackson, they'll talk."

"Get him out of here," DeMarco snarled.

The blue suits came toward me. I got out of there. I could use the smoke anyway.

8

I was closing my front door behind me when Rena came out of the bedroom. She had fixed her make-up since the last time I had seen her, but she had on the same navy suit and it was starting to look like a navy suit she had had on for two days.

I said, "You remembered to relock the door this time."

She nodded. "I stayed in a motel last night. The cops haven't got to them all yet. But I couldn't hang around. They get suspicious when you don't have luggage."

"You can't stay here. I just painted a bull's-eye on my back for Fred DeMarco." I told her what I'd told him.

"I can't identify the men who killed Dave," she protested.

"Freddy the Mark doesn't know that." I lifted the telephone. "I'm getting you a cab ride to Police Headquarters and then I'm calling the cops. Things are going to get interesting as soon as DeMarco gets over his mad."

The doorbell buzzed. This time I didn't have to tell her. She went into the bedroom and I got my Luger off the table and opened the door on a man who was a little shorter than I, with gray eyes like nickels on a pad. He had traded his Windbreaker for a brown leather jacket but it looked like the same .22 target pistol in his right hand. Without the ski mask he looked about my age, with streaks of premature gray in his neat brown hair.

I waved the Luger and said, "Mine's bigger."

"Old movie line," he said with a sigh. "Take a gander behind you."

That was an old movie line too. I didn't turn. Then someone gasped and I stepped back and moved my head just enough to get the corner of my eye working. A man a little taller than Gray Eyes, with black hair to his collar and a handlebar moustache, stood behind Rena this side of the bedroom door with a squat .38 planted against her neck. His other hand was out of sight and the way Rena was standing said he had her left arm twisted behind her back. He too had ditched his Windbreaker and was in shirtsleeves. The lighter caliber gun he had used on Tillet and probably on Paul Venito would be scrap by now.

It seemed I was the only one who needed a key to get into my house.

"Two beats one, Zorro." Gray Eyes' tone remained tired and I figured out that was his normal voice. He stepped over the threshold and leaned the door shut. "Let's have the Heine." He held out his free hand.

"Uh-uh," I said. "I give it to you and then you shoot us."

"You don't, we shoot the girl first. Then you."

"You'll do that anyway. This way maybe I shoot you too."

Moustache shifted his weight. Rena shrieked. My eyes flickered that way. Gray Eyes swept the barrel of the .22 across my face and grasped the end of the Luger. I fired. The report gulped up all the sound in the room. Moustache let go of Rena and swung the .38 my way. She knocked up his arm and red flame streaked ceilingward. Rena dived for her blue bag on the easy chair. Moustache aimed at her back. I swung the Luger, but Gray Eyes was still standing and fired the .22. Something plucked at my left bicep. The front window exploded then, and Moustache was lifted off his feet and flung backwards against the wall, his gun flying. The nasty cracking report followed an instant later.

I looked at Gray Eyes, but he was down now, his gun still in his hand but forgotten, both hands clasped over his abdomen with the blood dark between his fingers. I relieved him of the weapon and put it with the Luger on the table. Rena was half-reclining in the easy chair with her skirt hiked up over one long leg and her .32 Remington in both hands pointing at Moustache dead on the floor. She hadn't fired.

"Walker?"

The voice was tinny and artificially loud. But I recognized it.

"We're all right, John," I called. "Put down that bullhorn and come in." I told Rena to drop the automatic. She obeyed, in a daze.

Alderdyce came in with his gun drawn and looked at the man still alive at his feet and across at the other man who wasn't and at Rena. I introduced them. "She didn't set up Tillet," I added. "Fred DeMarco bought the hit, not Venito. This one will get around to telling you that if you stop gawking and call an ambulance before he's done bleeding into his belly."

"For you too, maybe." Alderdyce picked up the telephone. He'd seen me grasping my left arm. "Just a crease," I said. "Like in the cowboy pictures."

"You're lucky. I know you, Walker. It's your style to set yourself up as the goat to smoke out a guy like DeMarco. I had men watching the place and had you tailed to and from Great Lakes. When the girl broke in we loaded the neighborhood. Then these two showed —" He broke off and started speaking into the mouthpiece.

I said, "My timing was off. I'm glad yours was better."

The bearded black sergeant came in with some uniformed officers, one of whom carried a 30.06 rifle with a mounted scope. "Nice shooting," Alderdyce told him, hanging up. "What's your name?"

"Officer Carl Breen, Lieutenant." He spelled it.

"Okay."

I let go of my arm and wiped the blood off my hand with my handkerchief and got out my wallet, counting out two hundred and fifty dollars, which I held out to Rena. "My day rate's two-fifty."

She was sitting up now, looking at the money. "Why'd you ask for five hundred?"

"You had your mind made up about me. It saved a speech."

"Keep it. You earned it and a lot more than I can pay."

I folded the bills and stuck them inside the outer breast pocket of her navy jacket. "I'd just blow it on cigarettes and whisky."

"Who's the broad?" demanded the sergeant.

I thought of telling him that's what a Dulcinea was, but the joke was old. We waited for the ambulance.

The surviving gunman's name was Richard Bledsoe. He had two priors in the Detroit area for ADW, one conviction, and after he was released from the hospital into custody he turned state's evidence and convicted Fred DeMarco on two counts of conspiracy to commit murder. DeMarco's appeal is still pending. The dead man went by Austin Grant and had done seven years in San Quentin for second-degree homicide knocked down from Murder One. The Detroit Police worked a deal with the Justice Department and got Rena Murrow relocation and a new identity to shield her from DeMarco's friends. I never saw her again.

I never ate in Butch's diner again, either. These days you can't get in the place without a reservation.

I'm in the Book

1

WHEN I FINALLY GOT IN to see Alec Wynn of Reiner, Switz, Galsworthy, & Wynn, the sun was high over Lake St. Clair outside the window behind his desk and striking sparks off the choppy steel-blue surface with sailboats gliding around on it cutting white foam, their sharkfin sails striped in broad bright bikini colors. Wynn sat with his back to the view and never turned to look at it. He didn't need to. On the wall across from him hung a big framed color photograph of bright-striped sailboats cutting white foam on the steel-blue surface of Lake St. Clair.

Wynn was a big neat man with a black widow's peak trimmed tight to his skull and the soft gray hair at his temples worn long over the tops of his ears. He had on aviator's glasses with clear plastic rims and a suit the color and approximate weight of ground fog, that fit him like no suit will ever fit me if I hit the Michigan Lottery tomorrow. He had deep lines in his Miami-brown face and a mouth that turned down like a shark's to show a bottom row of caps as white and even as military monuments. It was a predator's face. I liked it fine. It belonged to a lawyer, and in my business lawyers mean a warm feeling in the pit of the bank account.

"Walker, Amos," he said, as if he were reading roll call. "I like the name. It has a certain smoky strength."

"I've had it a long time."

He looked at me with his strong white hands folded on top

of his absolutely clean desk. His palms didn't leave marks on the glossy surface the way mine would have. "I keep seeing your name on reports. The Reliance people employ your services often."

"Only when the job involves people," I said. "Those big investigation agencies are good with computers and diamonds and those teeny little cameras you can hide in your left ear. But when it comes to stroking old ladies who see things and leaning on supermarket stock boys who smuggle sides of beef out the back door, they remember us little shows."

"How big is your agency?"

"You're looking at it. I have an answering service," I added quickly.

"Better and better. It means you can keep a secret. You have a reputation for that, too."

"Who told?"

"The humor I can take or let alone." He refolded his hands the other way. "I don't like going behind Reliance's back like this. We've worked together for years and the director's an old friend. But this is a personal matter, and there are some things you would prefer to have a stranger know than someone you play poker with every Saturday night."

"I don't play poker," I said. "Whoops, sorry." I got out a cigarette and smoothed it between my fingers. "Who's missing, your wife or your daughter?"

He shot me a look he probably would have kept hooded in court. Then he sat back, nodding slightly. "I guess it's not all that uncommon."

"I do other work but my main specialty is tracing missing persons. You get so you smell it coming." I waited.

"It's my wife. She's left me again."

"Again?"

"Last time it was with one of the apprentices here, a man named Lloyd Debner. But they came back after three days. I fired him, naturally."

"Naturally."

A thin smile played around with his shark's mouth, gave it up and went away. "Seems awfully Old Testament, I know. I tried to be modern about it. There's really no sense in blaming the other man. But I saw myself hiding out in here to avoid meeting him in the hall, and that would be grotesque. I gave him excellent references. One of our competitors snapped him up right away."

"What about this time?"

"She left the usual note saying she was going away and I was not to look for her. I called Debner but he assured me he hadn't seen Cecelia since their first — fling. I believe him. But it's been almost a week now and I'm concerned for her safety."

"What about the police?"

"I believe we covered that when we were discussing keeping secrets," he said acidly.

"You've been married how long?"

"Six years. And, yes, she's younger than I, by fourteen years. That was your next question, wasn't it?"

"It was in there. Do you think that had anything to do with her leaving?"

"I think it had everything to do with it. She has appetites that I've been increasingly unable to fulfill. But I never thought it was a problem until she left the first time."

"You quarreled?"

"The normal amount. Never about that. Which I suppose is revealing. I rather think she's found a new boyfriend, but I'm damned if I can say who it is."

"May I see the note?"

He extracted a fold of paper from an inside breast pocket and passed it across the desk. "I'm afraid I got my fingerprints all over it before I thought over all the angles."

"That's okay. I never have worked on anything where prints were any use."

It was written on common drugstore stationery, tinted blue

with a spray of flowers in the upper right-hand corner. A hasty hand full of sharp points and closed loops. It said what he'd reported it had said and nothing else. Signed with a *C*.

"There's no date."

"She knew I'd read it the day she wrote it. It was last Tuesday."

"Uh-huh."

"That means what?" he demanded.

"Just uh-huh. It's something I say when I can't think of anything to say." I gave back the note. "Any ideas where she might go to be alone? Favorite vacation spot, her hometown, a summer house, anything like that? I don't mean to insult you. Sometimes the hardest place to find your hat is on your head."

"We sublet our Florida home in the off-season. She grew up in this area and has universally disliked every place we've visited on vacation. Really, I was expecting something more from a professional."

"I'm just groping for a handle. Does she have any hobbies?"

"Spending my money."

I watched my cigarette smoke drifting toward the window. "It seems to me you don't know your wife too well after six years, Mr. Wynn. When I find her, if I find her, I can tell you where she is, but I can't make her come back, and from the sound of things she may not want to come back. I wouldn't be representing your best interests if I didn't advise you to save your money and set the cops loose on it. I can't give guarantees they won't give."

"Are you saying you don't want the job?"

"Not me. I don't have any practice at that. Just being straight with a client I'd prefer keeping."

"Don't do me any favors, Walker."

"Okay. I'll need a picture. And what's her maiden name? She may go back to it."

"Collier." He spelled it. "And here." He got a wallet-size color photograph out of the top drawer of the desk and skidded it across the glossy top like someone dealing a card.

She was a redhead, and the top of that line. She looked like someone who would wind up married to a full partner in a weighty law firm with gray temples and an office overlooking Lake St. Clair. It would be in her high school yearbook under Predictions.

I put the picture in my breast pocket. "Where do I find this Debner?"

"He's with Paxton and Ring on West Michigan. But I told you he doesn't know where Cecelia is."

"Maybe he should be asked a different way." I killed my stub in the smoking stand next to the chair and rose. "You'll be hearing from me."

His eyes followed me up. All eight of his fingers were lined up on the near edge of his desk, the nails pink and perfect. "Can you be reached if I want to hear from you sooner?"

"My service will page me. I'm in the book."

2

A Japanese accent at Paxton & Ring told me over the telephone that Lloyd Debner would be tied up all afternoon in Detroit Recorder's Court. Lawyers are always in court the way executives are always in meetings. At the Frank Murphy Hall of Justice a bailiff stopped spitting on his handkerchief and rubbing at a spot on his uniform to point out a bearded man in his early thirties with a mane of black hair, smoking a pipe and talking to a gray-headed man in the corridor outside one of the courtrooms. I went over there and introduced myself.

"Second," he said, without taking his eyes off the other man. "Tim, we're talking a lousy twenty bucks over the fifteen hundred. Even if you win, the judge will order probation. The kid'll get that anyway if we plead Larceny Under, and there's no percentage in mucking up his record for life just to fatten your win column. And there's nothing saying you'll win."

I said, "This won't take long."

"Make an appointment. Listen, Tim —"

"It's about Cecelia Wynn," I said. "We can talk about it out here in the hall if you like. Tim won't mind."

He looked at me then for the first time. "Tim, I'll catch you later."

"After the sentencing." The gray-headed man went into the courtroom, chuckling.

"Who'd you say you were?" Debner demanded.

"Amos Walker. I still am, but a little older. I'm a P.I. Alec Wynn hired me to look for his wife."

"You came to the wrong place. That's all over."

"I'm interested in when it wasn't."

He glanced up and down the hall. There were a few people in it, lawyers and fixers and the bailiff with the stain that wouldn't go away from his crisp blue uniform shirt. "Come on. I can give you a couple of minutes."

I followed him into a men's room two doors down. We stared at a guy combing his hair in front of the long mirror over the sinks until he put away his comb and picked up a brown leather briefcase and left. Debner bent down to see if there were any feet in the stalls, straightened, and knocked out his pipe into a sink. He laid it on a soap canister to cool and moved his necktie a centimeter to the right.

"I don't see Cecelia when we pass on the street," he said, inspecting the results in the mirror. "I had my phone number changed after we got back from Jamaica so she couldn't call me."

"That where you went?"

"I rented a bungalow outside Kingston. Worst mistake I ever made. I was headed for a junior partnership at Reiner when this happened. Now I'm back to dealing school board presidents' sons out of jams they wouldn't be in if five guys ahead of me hadn't dealt them out of jams just like them starting when they were in junior high."

"How'd you and Cecelia get on?"

"Oh, swell. So good we crammed a two-week reservation into three days and came back home."

"What went wrong?"

"Different drummers." He picked up his pipe and blew through it.

"Not good enough," I said.

He grinned boyishly. "I didn't think so. To begin with, she's a health nut. I run and take a little wheat germ myself sometimes — you don't even have to point a gun at me — but I draw the line at dropping vitamins and herb pills at every meal. She must've taken sixteen capsules every time we sat down to eat. It can drive you blinkers. People in restaurants must've figured her for a drug addict."

"Sure she wasn't?"

"She was pretty open about taking them if she was. She filled the capsules herself from plastic bags. Her purse rattled like a used car."

A fat party in a gray suit and pink shirt came in and smiled and nodded at both of us and used the urinal and washed his hands. Debner used the time to recharge his pipe.

"Still not good enough," I said, when the fat party had gone. "You don't cut a vacation short just because your bedpartner does wild garlic."

"It just didn't work out. Look, I'm due back in court."

"Not at half-past noon." I waited.

He finished lighting his pipe, dropped the match into the sink where he'd knocked his ashes, grinned around the stem. I bet that melted the women jurors. "If this gets around I'm washed up with every pretty legal secretary in the building."

"Nothing has to get around. I'm just looking for Cecelia Wynn."

"Yeah. You said." He puffed on the pipe, took it out, smoothed his beard, and looked at it in the mirror. "Yeah. Well, she said she wasn't satisfied."

"Uh-huh."

"No one's ever told me that before. I'm not used to complaints."

"Uh-*huh*."

He turned back toward me. His eyes flicked up and down. "We never had this conversation, okay?"

"What conversation?"

"Yeah." He put the pipe back between his teeth, puffed. "Yeah."

We shook hands. He squeezed a little harder than I figured he did normally.

3

I dropped two dimes into a pay telephone in the downstairs lobby and fought my way through two secretaries before Alec Wynn came on the line. His voice was a full octave deeper than it had been in person. I figured it was that way in court too.

"Just checking back, Mr. Wynn. How come when I asked you about hobbies you didn't tell me your wife was into herbs?"

"Into *what?*"

I told him what Debner had said about the capsules. He said, "I haven't dined with my wife in months. Most legal business is conducted in restaurants."

"I guess you wouldn't know who her herbalist is, then."

"Herbalist?"

"Sort of an oregano guru. They tell their customers which herbs to take in the never-ending American quest for a healthy body. Not a few of the runaways I've traced take their restlessness to them first."

"Well, I wouldn't know anything about that. Trina might. Our maid. She's at the house now."

"Would you call her and tell her I'm coming?"
He said he would and broke the connection.

4

It was a nice place if you like windows. There must have been fifty on the street side alone, with ivy or something just as green crawling up the brick wall around them and a courtyard with a marble fountain in the center and a black chauffeur with no shirt on washing a blue Mercedes in front. They are always washing cars. A white-haired Puerto Rican woman with muddy eyes and a faint moustache answered my ring.

"Trina?"

"Yes. You are Mr. Walker? Mr. Wynn told me to expect you."

I followed her through a room twice the size of my living room, but that was designed just for following maids through, and down a hall with dark paintings on the walls to a glassed-in porch at the back of the house containing ferns in pots and lawn chairs upholstered in floral print. The sliding glass door leading outside was ajar and a strong chlorine stench floated in from an outdoor crescent-shaped swimming pool. She slid the door shut.

"The pool man says alkali is leaking into the water from an underground spring," she said. "The chlorine controls the smell."

"The rich suffer too." I told her what I wanted.

"Capsules? Yes, Mrs. Wynn has many bottles of capsules in her room. There is a name on the bottles. I will get one."

"No hurry. What sort of woman is Mrs. Wynn to work for?"

"I don't know that that is a good question to answer."

"You're a good maid, Trina." I wound a five-dollar bill around my right index finger.

She slid the tube off the finger and flattened it and folded it over and tucked it inside her apron pocket. "She is a good employer. She says please and does not run her fingers over the furniture after I have dusted, like the last woman I worked for."

"Is that all you can tell me?"

"I have not worked here long, sir. Only five weeks."

"Who was maid before that?"

"A girl named Ann Foster, at my agency. Multi-Urban Services. She was fired." Her voice sank to a whisper on the last part. We were alone.

"Fired why?"

"William the chauffeur told me she was fired. I didn't ask why. I have been a maid long enough to learn that the less you know the more you work. I will get one of the bottles."

She left me, returning a few minutes later carrying a glass container the size of an aspirin bottle, with a cork in the top. It was half full of gelatin capsules filled with fine brown powder. I pulled the cork and sniffed. A sharp, spicy scent. The name of a health foods store on Livernois was typewritten on the label.

"How many of these does Mrs. Wynn have in her bedroom?" I asked.

"Many. Ten or twelve bottles."

"As full as this?"

"More, some of them."

"That's a lot of capsules to fill and then leave behind. Did she take many clothes with her?"

"No, sir. Her closets and drawers are full."

I thanked her and gave her back the bottle. It was getting to be the damnedest disappearing act I had covered in a long, long time.

The black chauffeur was hosing off the Mercedes when I came out. He was tall, almost my height, and the bluish skin of his torso was stretched taut over lumpy muscle. I asked him if he was William.

He twisted shut the nozzle of the hose, watching me from under his brows with his head down, like a boxer. Scar tissue shone around his eyes. "Depends on who you might be."

I sighed. When you can't even get their name out of them, the rest is like pulling nails with your toes. I stood a folded ten-spot on the Mercedes' hood. He watched the bottom edge darken as it soaked up water. "Ann Foster," I said.

"What about her?"

"How close was she to Cecelia Wynn?"

"I wouldn't know. I work outside."

"Who fired her, Mr. or Mrs. Wynn?"

He thought about it. Watched the bill getting wetter. Then he snatched it up and waved it dry. "She did. Mrs. Wynn."

"Why?"

He shrugged. I reached up and plucked the bill out of his fingers. He grabbed for it but I drew it back out of his reach. He shrugged again, wringing the hose in his hands to make his muscles bulge. "They had a fight of some kind the day Ann left. I could hear them screaming at each other out here. I don't know what it was about."

"Where'd she go after she left here?"

He started to shrug a third time, stopped. "Back to the agency, maybe. I don't ask questions. In this line —"

"Yeah. The less you know the more you work." I gave him the ten and split.

5

The health foods place was standard, plank floor and hanging plants and stuff you can buy in any supermarket for a fraction of what they were asking. The herbalist was a small, pretty woman of about 30, in a gypsy blouse and floor-length denim skirt with bare feet poking out underneath and a bandana tied around her head. She also owned the place. She hadn't seen

Mrs. Wynn since before she'd turned up missing. I bought a package of unsalted nuts for her trouble and ate them on the way to the office. They needed salt.

I found Multi-Urban Services in the Detroit metropolitan directory and dialed the number. A woman whose voice reminded me of the way cool green mints taste answered.

"We're not at liberty to give out information about our clients."

"I'm sorry to hear that," I said. "I went to a party at the Wynn place in Grosse Pointe about six weeks ago and was very impressed with Miss Foster's efficiency. I'd heard she was free and was thinking of engaging her services on a full-time basis."

The mints melted. "I'm sorry, Miss Foster is no longer with this agency. But I can recommend another girl just as efficient. Multi-Urban prides itself —"

"I'm sure it does. Can you tell me where Miss Foster is currently working?"

"Stormy Heat Productions. But not as a maid."

I thanked her and hung up, thinking about how little it takes to turn mint to acid. Stormy Heat was listed on Mt. Elliott. Its line was busy. Before leaving the office, I broke the Smith & Wesson out of the desk drawer and snapped the holster onto my belt under my jacket. It was that kind of neighborhood.

6

The outfit worked out of an old gymnasium across from Mt. Elliott Cemetery, a scorched brick building as old as the eight-hour day with a hand-lettered sign over the door and a concrete stoop deep in the process of going back to the land. The door was locked. I pushed a sunken button that grated in its socket. No sound issued from within. I was about to knock when a square panel opened in the door at head level and a mean black face with a beard that grew to a point looked into mine.

"You've got to be kidding," I said.

"What do you want?" demanded the face.

"Ann Foster."

"What for?"

"Talk."

"Sorry." The panel slid shut.

I was smoking a cigarette. I dropped it to the stoop and crushed it out and used the button again. When the panel shot back I reached up and grasped the beard in my fist and yanked. His chest banged the door.

"You white —!"

I twisted the beard in my fist. He gasped and tears sprang to his eyes. "Joe sent me," I said. "The goose flies high. May the Force be with you. Pick the password you like, but open the door."

"Who —?"

"Jerk Root, the Painless Barber. Open."

"Okay, okay." Metal snapped on his side. Still hanging on to his whiskers, I reached down with my free hand and tried the knob. It turned. I let go and opened the door. He was standing just inside the threshold, a big man in threadbare jeans and a white shirt open to the navel Byron-fashion, smoothing his beard with thick fingers. He had a Colt magnum in his other hand pointed at my belt buckle.

"Nice," I said. "The nickel plating goes with your eyes. You got a permit for that?"

He smiled crookedly. His eyes were still watering. "Why didn't you say you was cop?" He reached back and jammed the revolver into a hip pocket. "You got paper?"

"Not today. I'm not raiding the place. I just want to talk to Ann Foster."

"Okay," he said. "Okay. I don't need no beef with the laws. You don't see nothing on the way, deal?"

I spread my hands. "I'm blind. This isn't an election year."

There was a lot not to see. Films produced by Stormy Heat were not interested in the Academy Award or even feature billing at the all-night grindhouses on Woodward Avenue. Its actors were thin and ferretlike and its actresses used powder to fill the cavities in their faces and cover their stretch marks. The lights and cameras were strictly surplus, their cables frayed and patched all over like old garden hoses. We walked past carnal scenes, unnoticed by the grunting performers or the sweat-stained crews, to a scuffed steel door at the rear that had originally led into a locker room. My escort went through it without pausing. I followed.

"Don't they teach you to knock in the jungle?"

I'd had a flash of a naked youthful brown body, and then it was covered by a red silk kimono that left a pair of long legs bare to the tops of the thighs. She had her hair cut very short and her face, with its upturned nose and lower lip thrust out in a belligerent pout, was boyish. I had seen enough to know she wasn't a boy.

"What's to see that I ain't already seen out on the floor?" asked the Beard. "Man to see you. From the Machine."

Ann Foster looked at me quickly. The whites of her eyes had a bluish tinge against her dark skin. "Since when they picking matinee idols for cops?"

"Thanks," I said. "But I've got a job."

We stared at the guy with the beard until he left us, letting the door drift shut behind him. The room had been converted into a community dressing room, but without much conviction. A library table littered with combs and brushes and pots of industrial strength make-up stood before a long mirror, but the bench on this side had come with the place and the air smelled of mildew and old sweat. She said, "Show me you're cop."

I flashed my photostat and honorary sheriff's star. "I'm private. I let Lothar out there think different. It saved time."

"Well, you wasted it all here. I don't like rental heat any more than the other kind. I don't even like men."

"You picked a swell business not to like them in."

She smiled, not unpleasantly. "I work with an all-girl cast."

"Does it pay better than being a maid?"

"About as much. But when I get on my knees it's not to scrub floors."

"Cecelia Wynn," I said.

Her face moved as if I'd slapped her. "What about her?" she barked.

"She's missing. Her husband wants her back. You had a fight with her just before you got fired. What started it?"

"What happens if I don't answer?"

"Nothing. Now. But if it turns out she doesn't want to be missing, the cops get it. I could save you a trip downtown."

She said, "Hell, she's probably off someplace with her lawyer boyfriend like last time."

"No, he's accounted for. Also she left almost all her clothes behind, along with the herbs she spent a small country buying and a lot of time stuffing into capsules. It's starting to look like leaving wasn't her idea, or that where she was going she wouldn't need those things. What was the fight about?"

"I wouldn't do windows."

I slapped her for real. It made a loud flat noise off the echoing walls and she yelled. The door swung open. Beard stuck his face inside. Farther down the magnum glittered. "What."

I looked at him, looked at the woman. She stroked her burning cheek. My revolver was behind my right hipbone, a thousand miles away. Finally she said, "Nothing."

"Sure?"

She nodded. The man with the beard left his eyes on me a moment longer, then withdrew. The door closed.

"It was weird," she told me. "Serving dinner this one night I spilled salad oil down the front of my uniform. I went to my room to change. Mrs. Wynn stepped inside to ask for something, just like you walked in on me just now. She caught me naked."

"So?"

"So she excused herself and got out. Half an hour later I was canned. For spilling the salad oil. I yelled about it, as who wouldn't? But it wasn't the reason."

"What was?"

She smoothed the kimono across her pelvis. "You think I don't know that look on another woman's face when I see it?"

We talked some more, but none of it was for me. On my way out I laid a twenty on the dressing table and stood a pot of mascara on top of it. I hesitated, then added one of my cards to the stack. "In case something happens to change your mind about rental heat," I said. "If you lose the card, I'm in the book."

Back in civilization I gassed up and used the telephone in the service station to call Alec Wynn at his office. I asked him to meet me at his home in Grosse Pointe in twenty minutes.

"I can't," he said. "I'm meeting a client at four."

"He'll keep. If you don't show you may be one yourself."
We stopped talking to each other.

7

Both William the chauffeur and the Mercedes were gone from the courtyard, leaving only a puddle on the asphalt to reflect the window-studded façade of the big house. Trina let me in and listened to me and escorted me back to the enclosed porch. When she left I slid open the glass door and stepped outside to the pool area. I was there when Wynn came out five minutes later. His gray suit looked right even in those surroundings. It always would.

"You've caused me to place an important case in the hands

of an apprentice," he announced. "I hope this means you've found Cecelia."

"I've found her. I think."

"What's that supposed to signify? Or is this the famous Walker sense of humor at work?"

"Save it for your next jury, Mr. Wynn. We're just two guys talking. How long have you been hanging on to your wife's good-bye note? Since the first time she walked out?"

"You're babbling."

"It worried me that it wasn't dated," I said. "A thing like that comes in handy too often. Being in corporate law, you might not know that the cops have ways now to treat writing in ink with chemicals that can prove within a number of weeks when it was written."

His face was starting to match his suit. I went on.

"Someone else knew you hadn't been able to satisfy Cecelia sexually, or you wouldn't have been so quick to tell me. Masculine pride is a strong motive for murder, and in case something had happened to her, you wanted to be sure you were covered. That's why you hired me, and that's why you dusted off the old note. She didn't leave one this time, did she?"

"You have found her."

I said nothing. Suddenly he was an old man. He shuffled blindly to a marble bench near the pool and sank down onto it. His hands worked on his knees.

"When I didn't hear from her after several days I became frightened," he said. "The servants knew we argued. She'd told Debner of my — shortcomings. Before I left criminal law, I saw several convictions obtained on flimsier evidence. Can you understand that I had to protect myself?"

I said, "It wasn't necessary. Debner was just as unsuccessful keeping her happy. Any man would have been. Your wife was a lesbian, Mr. Wynn."

"That's a damn lie!" He started to rise. Halfway up, his knees gave out and he sat back down with a thud.

"Not a practicing one. It's possible she didn't even realize what her problem was until about five weeks ago, when she accidentally saw your former maid naked. The maid is a lesbian and recognized the reaction. Was Cecelia a proud woman?"

"Intensely."

"A lot of smoke gets blown about the male fear of loss of masculinity," I said. "No one gives much thought to women's fears for their femininity. They can drive a woman to fire a servant out of hand, but she would just be removing temptation from her path for the moment. After a time, when the full force of her situation struck home, she might do something more desperate.

"She would be too proud to leave a note."

Wynn had his elbows on his knees and his face in his hands. I peeled cellophane off a fresh pack of Winstons.

"The cops can't really tell when a note was written, Mr. Wynn. I just said that to hear what you'd say."

"Where is she, Walker?"

I watched my reflection in the pool's turquoise-colored surface, squinting against the chlorine fumes. The water was clear enough to see through to the bottom, but there was a recessed area along the north edge with a shelf obscuring it from above, a design flaw that would trap leaves and twigs and other debris that would normally be exposed when the pool was drained. Shadows swirled in the pocket, thick and dark and full of secrets.

Bodyguards
Shoot Second

"A. WALKER INVESTIGATIONS."

"Amos Walker?"

The voice on the other end of the line was male and youthful, one of those that don't change from the time they crack until the time they quake. I said, "This is he."

"Huh?"

"Grammar," I said. "It gets me business in Grosse Pointe. But not lately. Who's speaking?"

"This is Martin Cole. I'm Billy Dickerson's road manager."

"Okay."

"No, really."

"I believe you, Mr. Martin. How can I make your life easier?"

"Cole. Martin's my first name. Art Cradshaw recommended you. He said you were the best man for what you do in Detroit."

"Sweet of him. But he still owes me for the credit check I ran for his company six months ago."

"That's hardly my business. I need a man."

I parked the receiver in the hollow of my shoulder and lit a Winston.

"Walker?"

"I'm here. You need a man."

"The man I need doesn't pick his teeth with his thumbnail and can wear a dinner jacket without looking as if he was strapped in waiting for the current, but doesn't worry about popping a seam when he has to push somebody's face in. He's a good enough shot to light a match at thirty paces on no notice, but he carries himself as if he thought the butt of a gun would spoil the lines of his suit. He can swear and spit when called upon but in polite conversation wouldn't split an infinitive at knifepoint."

I said, "I wish you'd let me know when you find him. I could use someone like that in the investigation business."

"According to Art Cradshaw you're that man."

"I don't own a dinner jacket, Mr. Dickerson."

"Cole. Dickerson's the man I represent. The jacket's no problem. We have a tailor traveling with us and he'll fix you up in a day."

"I didn't know tailors traveled. But then I don't know any tailors. What business are you and Mr. Dickerson in?"

Pause. "You're kidding, right?"

"Probably not. I don't have a sense of humor."

"Billy Dickerson. The singer. Rock and Country. He's open-ing at the Royal Tower in Dearborn tomorrow night. Don't tell me you've never heard of him."

"My musical appreciation stops around nineteen sixty-two. What sort of work do you have in mind for this cross between Richard Gere and the Incredible Hulk?"

"Protection. Billy's regular bodyguard has disappeared and he can't leave his suite here at the Tower without someone to stand between him and his adoring fans. Too much adoration can be fatal."

"I don't do that kind of work, Mr. Cole. Bodyguards shoot second. If at all."

"We're paying a thousand. For the week."

I hesitated. Habit. Then: "My daily's two-fifty. That comes to seventeen-fifty for seven days."

"We'll go that."

"Can't do it, Mr. Cole. I'm sitting on retainer for a local union just now. They could call me anytime. Try Ned Eccles on Michigan; security's his specialty. Infinitives don't last too long around him, but he's hard and fast and he knows how to tie a bow.''

"I don't know. Art said you were the guy to call.''

"Cradshaw's in the tool design business. He doesn't know a bodyguard from a right cross.''

"I thought you guys never turned down a job.''

I said, "It's not a thing I'd care to get good at. Tell Ned I sent you.''

"Will he give me a discount?''

"No. But he might give me one next time I farm something out to him.'' I wished him good luck and we were through talking to each other.

The union rep didn't call that day or the next, just as he hadn't called for a week, not since the day I'd accepted his retainer. Meanwhile I was laying in a hundred and a half every twenty-four hours just for playing solitaire within reach of the telephone. I closed the office at five and drove home. It was November. The city was stone-colored under a gray sky and in the air was the raw-iron smell that comes just before a snow.

Out of long habit I flipped on the television set the minute I got in the door and went into the kitchen, stripping off my jacket and tie as I went. When I came out opening a can of beer the picture had come on but not the sound and I was looking at a studio shot of Ned Eccles' fleshy moustached face.

". . . died three hours later at Detroit Receiving Hospital,'' came on the announcer's voice, too loud. I jumped and turned down the volume. Now they were showing film of a lean young man in a gold lamé jumpsuit unzipped to his pelvis and stringy blond hair to his shoulders striding down a stage runway, shouting song lyrics into a hand mike while the crowd jammed up against the footlights screamed. The announcer continued.

"Dickerson, shown here during his last appearance at the Royal Tower two years ago, was shoved out of the line of fire by a member of his entourage after the first shot and was unharmed. The slain bodyguard has been identified as Edward Eccles, forty-five, a Detroit private investigator with a background in personal security. Police have no leads as yet to the man who fired the shots." After a short pause during which the camera focused on the announcer's grave face, he turned his head and smiled. "How are the Tigers doing, Steve?"

I changed channels. There was a commercial for a women's hygiene product on the next local station and a guy in a chef's hat showing how to make cheese gooey on the last. I turned off the set and sipped beer and thought. The telephone interrupted my thinking.

"Walker?"

"Yeah."

"This is Carol Greene. You heard?"

Carol Greene was Ned Eccles' business partner. I said, "I just caught a piece of it. What happened?"

"Not on the phone. Can you come to Ned's office?"

"What for?"

"I'll tell you when you get here." After a beat: "You owe Ned. You got him killed."

"Don't hang that on me, Carol. I just made a referral. He didn't have to take the job. Give me twenty minutes." I hung up and retrieved my tie and jacket.

2

Eccles Investigations and Security worked out of a storefront off Cadillac Square, with an oak railing separating Carol's desk in front from Ned's in back and a lot of framed photographs on the walls of Ned shaking hands with the mayor and the governor and various presidential candidates whose faces remained vaguely familiar long after their names were faded on old baled ballots. The place had a friendly, informal, unfussy look that had set its owners back at least three grand. The basement vault where the firm's files were kept had cost more than the building. I went through a swinging gate in the railing to Ned's desk where Carol was supporting herself on her small angular fists.

"Give some guys twenty minutes and they'll take forty," she greeted.

"The rush hour got me by the throat. You look the same as always."

"Don't start." She put the cigarette she was holding between thumb and forefinger to her lips, bit off some smoke, and tipped it down her throat in a series of short, jerky movements like a bird bolting grain. She was a small, wiry woman in a man's flannel shirt and jeans with gray-streaked blond hair cut very short and unadorned glasses with underslung bows. She had been Ned Eccles' junior partner for ten years. Whatever else she might have been to him wasn't my business today or ever.

"How much do you know about what happened to Ned?" she asked.

"Just that he was killed. Apparently by someone trying to get Billy Dickerson."

She nodded jerkily, ate some more cigarette, ground it out in a glass ashtray full of butts on the desk. "Dickerson stopped to sign an autograph in front of the service elevator on the way up to his suite at the Royal Tower. Ned had told him to avoid the lobby. He'd told him not to stop for anyone either, but I guess Billy-boy didn't hear that part. The guy ducked Ned and stuck a pad in Dickerson's hand and while Dickerson was getting out a pen he pulled a piece. Ned saw it and got between them just in time to get his guts drilled. That was about noon. He spent the afternoon dying. I just got back from the hospital."

Her eyes were a little red behind the cheaters. I said, "Who saw this?"

"Dickerson's manager, Martin Cole. Dickerson. Some gofer, Phil something. I talked to them at the hospital. While they were busy getting the Music Man out of the way of the bullets the gunny lit out through the rear entrance. Six feet, a hundred and eighty, thirties, balding. Dark zipper jacket. That's as good as it gets. The croakers dug two thirty-eight slugs out of Ned's insides."

"Say anything before he died?"

She shook her head, firing up a fresh cigarette from a butane lighter whose flame leaped halfway to the ceiling. "Outside of cussing a blue streak. That why you turned Cole down? You had dope on the shoot?"

"I was in the clutch when he called."

"Yeah."

I said, "Ned and I didn't get along, that's yesterday's news. We had different ideas about how the investigating business should be run. But I didn't put him in front of those bullets."

"Yeah. I guess not." She tossed the cold lighter atop a stack of Manila file folders on the desk. Then she looked at me. "I'll go your full rate to look into Ned's death."

"Ned's death was an accident."

"Maybe. Either way you get paid."

"You've got a license."

"I make out the books, trace an occasional skip. That's all I've done for ten years. Ned was the detective. You do this kind of thing all the time."

"Wrong. Mostly I look for missing persons."

"The guy who killed Ned is missing."

"He's cop meat," I said. "Save your money and let them do their job."

"Cops. First Monday of every month I hand an envelope to our department pipeline, a night captain. A thing like that can shake your faith. You still in the clutch?"

I nodded. "Retainer. I sit by the telephone."

"You've got an answering service to do that. Look, I won't beg you." She made a face and killed the butt, smoked only a third down. "I know everyone thought I was sleeping with Ned, including that slut of a wife of his, who should know about that kind of thing. I haven't cared what people thought of me since my senior prom. For the record, though, I wasn't.

He was my friend and my partner and I have to do this one thing for him before I can go back to what I was doing. If you won't take the job I'll find someone else. The Yellow Pages are lousy with plastic badges."

"I'll look into it. Courtesy rate, two hundred a day and expenses. Couple of days should tell if I'm wasting your money."

She wrote out a check for five hundred dollars and gave it to me. "That should see you through. If it doesn't, come back here. With an itemized list of expenses. No whiskey."

"You keep the books, all right." I folded the check and stuck it in my wallet. "One question. Don't hit me with the desk when I ask it."

"Ask."

"Did you ever know Ned to be the kind of a bodyguard who would throw himself between a gun and its target, even if the target was the person he was guarding?"

"No," she said quickly. "No, I didn't know him to be that kind of a bodyguard."

"Neither did I."

3

I cashed the check at my bank, deposited all but a hundred of it, and drove the four miles to Dearborn. The sky was low and the heater took ten minutes to chase the chill out of the upholstery. I parked in the lot behind the Royal Tower. A uniformed cop stopped me at the main entrance to the hotel. "Excuse me, sir, but are you a guest here?"

"No, I'm here to see someone."

"No one goes in without a room key, sorry. We had some excitement here earlier."

I handed him one of my cards. "Would you see that Martin Cole gets that? He's with Billy Dickerson. It's important."

The cop called over another uniform, gave him the card,

and told him to take it up. Ten minutes later the second officer returned. "Lieutenant says okay." To me: "Three-oh-six."

More uniforms and a group of men in suits greeted me in the hall when I stepped off the elevator. One of the latter was an inch shorter than I but half again as broad through the shoulders. It would have been a long time since he had gone through a doorway any way but sideways. His skin was pale to the point of translucence, almost albino, but his eyes were blue. He combed his short blond hair forward over a retreating widow's peak.

"Walker? I'm Gritch, homicide lieutenant with the Dearborn Police." He flashed his badge in a leather folder. "Cole says to let you through, but we got to check you for weapons."

"I'm not carrying," I said, but stood for the frisk by a black officer with hands like Ping-Pong paddles. Gritch meanwhile looked through the credentials in my wallet. He handed it back.

"Okay. We got to play it tight. The description of the guy that tried to kill Dickerson fits you as good as it fits a thousand other guys in this town."

"Anything new?" I put the crease back in my topcoat.

"Now, would I be earning your tax dollars if I answered that, after going to so much trouble to keep the public off the premises?"

"Nothing new," I said. "I thought so. Where's three-oh-six?"

"Right in front of you, Sherlock." He stepped away from it.

Before I could knock, the door was opened by a young man in shirtsleeves and stockinged feet. His hair was brown and wavy and combed behind his ears, his face clean-shaven, and his eyes as lifelike as two stones. He had a nine-millimeter automatic pistol in his right hand.

"Let him in, Phil."

The man who spoke was smaller than Lieutenant Gritch but not so small as Carol Greene, with a great mane of styled black hair and a drooping moustache and aviator's glasses with rose-tinted lenses. He wore a dark European-looking jacket with narrow lapels and a pinched waist over yellow-and-red checked pants. His shoes were brown leather with tassels, and he had a yellow silk scarf knotted at his throat. "Walker, is it? I'm Martin Cole. Decent of you to stop in."

At first glance, Cole was as youthful as his voice, but there were hairline fissures around his eyes and pouches at the corners of his mouth that his moustache couldn't hide. I took the moist warm hand he offered and entered the suite. The room was plushly carpeted and furnished as a living room, with a sofa and easy chairs, but folding metal chairs had been added. Cole caught me looking at them.

"For the press," he said. "We're holding a conference as soon as the police finish downstairs. Billy Dickerson, Amos Walker."

I looked at the man seated on the end of the sofa with a small barrel glass of copper-colored liquid in one hand. In person he was older and not so lean as he appeared on television. His skin was grayish against the long open collar of his white jumpsuit, and a distinct roll showed over his wide brown tooled-leather belt with an ornate gold buckle. His long yellow hair was thinning at the temples. He glanced at me, drank from his glass, and looked at Cole. "He the best you could do?"

"Walker came on his own, Billy," the manager said. Quickly he introduced the man with the gun as Phil Scabarda.

I said, "He must have a permit for that or he wouldn't be waving it around with the cops so close. That doesn't mean he can point it at me."

Cole gestured at the young man, who hesitated, then hung the pistol on a clip on the back of his belt. "Phil is Billy's driver and companion. These days that requires courses in racing and weaponry."

"Ned Eccles' partner hired me to look into the shooting," I said. "I appreciate your seeing me."

"Ah. I thought maybe you wanted his job after all. I'd rather hoped."

"You've got police protection now. What happened in front of the service elevator?"

"Well, we were standing there waiting for the doors to open when this guy came out from behind the elevator and asked Billy for his autograph. As soon as he got rid of the pad he pulled a gun from under his jacket. Eccles stepped in and took both bullets."

"Was Eccles armed?"

Cole nodded. "A revolver of some kind. I don't know from guns. It was still in his shoulder holster when the police came. There wasn't time to get it out."

"What was Phil doing while all this was going on?"

"Hustling Billy out of the way, with me. Meanwhile the guy got away." He gave me the same description he'd given Carol.

"If he was after Dickerson, why'd he leave without scratching him?"

"He panicked. Those shots were very loud in that enclosed space. As it was he barely got out before the place was jammed with gawkers."

"What happened to the pad?"

"Pad?"

"The pad he handed Dickerson for his autograph. Fingerprints."

"I guess Billy dropped it in the scramble. Some souvenir hunter has it by now."

I got out a cigarette and tapped it on the back of my left hand. "Anyone threaten Dickerson's life lately?"

"The police asked that. He gets his share of hate mail like every other big-name entertainer. They don't like his hair or his singing or his politics. That kind of letter is usually scribbled in Crayola on ruled paper with the lines an inch apart. I called Billy's secretary in L.A. to go through the files and send the most likely ones by air express for the police to look at. But she throws most of them away."

"What's the story on this bodyguard that disappeared?"

"Henry?" Carefully plucked eyebrows slid above the tinted glasses. "Forget him. He was a drunk and he got to wandering just when we needed him most. Flying in from L.A. day before yesterday we changed planes in Denver and he was missing when we boarded for Detroit. Probably found himself a bar and he's drying out in some drunk tank by now. If he hadn't ducked out we'd have fired him soon anyway. He was worse than no protection at all."

"Full name and description." I got out my notebook and pencil.

"Henry Bliss. About your height, a little over six feet. Two hundred pounds, sandy hair, fair complexion. Forty. Let's see, he had a white scar about an inch long on the right side of his jaw. Dropped his guard, he said. Don't waste your time with him. He was just an ex-pug with a taste for booze."

"It's my client's time. Any reason why someone would want to kill Dickerson? Besides his hair and his singing and his politics?"

"Celebrities make good clay pigeons. They're easier to get at than politicians, but you can become just as famous shooting them."

"Everyone's famous today. It's almost worth it to get an obscure person's autograph." I flipped the notebook shut. "Can I reach you here if something turns up?"

"We're booked downstairs for two weeks."

"Except for tonight."

"We're opening tonight as scheduled. Look, you can tell Ned's partner how sorry we are, but —"

"The show must go on."

Cole smiled thinly. "An ancient tradition with a solid mercenary base. No one likes giving refunds."

"Thanks, Mr. Cole. You'll be hearing from me."

"You know," he said, "I can't help thinking that had you been on the job, things would have gone differently today."

"Probably not. Ned knew his business. Your boy's alive. That's what you paid for."

As I closed the door behind me, Lieutenant Gritch came away from his crew next to the elevator. "What'd you get?" he demanded.

"Now, would I be earning my client's money if I answered that, after going to so much trouble to keep the cops out of my pockets?"

His pale face flushed for a moment. Then the color faded and he showed his eyeteeth in a gargoyle's grin, nodding. "Okay. I guess I bought that. We'll trade. You go."

I told him what I'd learned. He went on nodding.

"That's what we got. There's nothing in that autograph pad. Even if it had liftable prints, which nothing like that ever does, they'd have someone else's all over them by now. We Telexed this Henry Bliss's name and description to Denver. It won't buy zilch. This one's local and sloppy. If we get the guy at all it'll be because somebody unzipped his big yap. Give me a pro any time. These amateurs are a blank order."

"What makes him an amateur?"

"You mean besides he got the wrong guy? The gun. We frisked the service area and the parking lot and the alley next door. No gun. A pro would've used a piece without a history and then dumped it. He wouldn't take a chance on being picked up for CCW. You got a reference?"

The change of subjects threw me for a second. Then I gave him John Alderdyce's name in Detroit Homicide. He had a uniform write down the name in his notebook.

"Okay, we'll check you out. You know what the penalty is for interfering with a murder investigation."

"Something short of electrocution," I said. "In this state, anyway."

"Then I won't waste breath warning you off this one. You get anything — anything — you know where to come." He handed me one of his cards.

I gave him one of mine. "If you ever have a rug that needs looking under."

"I'd sooner put my gun in my mouth," he said. But he stuck the card in his pocket.

4

The sun had gone down, sucking all the heat out of the air. It still smelled like snow. On my way home I stopped at the main branch of the Detroit Public Library on Woodward, where I knew the security guard. I spotted him a ten to let me in after closing and browsed through the out-of-town directories until I found a list of detective agencies in Denver and copied some likelies into my notebook.

Colorado is two hours behind Michigan. Calling long-distance from home I found most of the offices still open. The first two I called didn't believe in courtesy rates. The third took down the information I had on Henry Bliss the wandering bodyguard and said they'd get back to me. I hung up and dialed my service for messages. I had a message. I got the union executive I was working for at home. He had a tail job for me, a shop steward suspected of pocketing membership dues.

"What am I looking for?" I asked.

"Where he goes with the money." The executive's tone was as smooth as ice. No lead pipes across his throat like in the old days. "He's not depositing it and he's not investing it. Follow him until it changes hands. Get pictures."

The job would start in the morning. I took down the necessary information, pegged the receiver, slid a TV tray into the oven, and mixed myself a drink while it was heating up. I felt like a pretty, empty-headed girl with two dates for Saturday night.

In the morning after breakfast I rang up Barry Stackpole at the Detroit *News*. While waiting for him to answer I watched the snow floating down outside the window turn brown before it reached the ground.

"Amos the famous shamus," said Barry, after I'd announced myself. "What can I do you for this lovely morning?"

"You must be in St. Tropez. I need a name on a pro heavy-weight." I described Ned Eccles' killer. Barry wrote a syndicated column on organized crime and had a national reputation and an artificial leg to show for it.

"Offhand I could name twenty that would fit," he said. "Local?"

"Maybe. More likely he was recruited from somewhere else."

"Make that a hundred. I can get a list to your office by special messenger this afternoon. What's the hit?"

"A P.I. named Eccles. You wouldn't know him. He ate that lead that was meant for Billy Dickerson yesterday."

"That was a hit?"

"I don't know. But the cops are following the amateur theory and that leaves this way open. I step on fewer official toes."

"When did you get religion?"

"I'm duplicating them on one thing, a previous bodyguard that got himself lost out West. The cops don't put much faith in it. I wouldn't be earning my fee if all I did was sniff their coattails. What's this list going to run me?"

"A fifth of Teacher's."

"Just one?"

"I'm cutting down. Hang tight."

After he broke the connection I called my service and asked them to page me if Denver called. Then I dug my little pen-size beeper out of a drawer full of spent cartridges and illegible notes to myself and clipped it to my belt and went to work for the union.

The shop steward lived a boring life. I tailed his Buick from his home in Redford Township to the GM Tech Center in Warren where he worked, picked him up again when he and two fellow workers walked downtown for lunch, ate in a booth across the restaurant from their table, and followed them back to work. One of the other guys got the tab. My guy took care of the tip. On my way out I glanced at the bills on the table. Two singles. He wasn't throwing the stuff away, that was sure.

During the long gray period before quitting time I found a public booth within sight of the Buick in the parking lot and called my service. There were no messages from Denver or anywhere else. I had the girl page me to see if the beeper was working. It was.

I followed the steward home, parked next to the curb for two hours waiting to see if he came out again, and when he didn't I started the engine and drove to the office. Opening the unlocked door of my little waiting room I smelled cop. The door to my private office, which I keep locked when I'm not in it, was standing open. I went through it and found Gritch sitting behind my desk looking at a sheet of typing paper. His skin wasn't any more colorful and he looked like a billboard with the window at his back. My Scotch bottle and one of my pony glasses stood on the desk, the glass half full.

"Pour one for me." I hung up my hat and coat.

He got the other glass out of the file drawer and filled it. His eyes didn't move from the paper in his left hand. "You got better taste in liquor than you do in locks," he said, leveling off his own glass.

"I'm working. I wasn't when I bought the lock." I put down my drink in one installment and waited for the heat to rise.

"This is quite a list you got. Packy Davis, yeah. Benny Boom-Boom Bohannen, sure. Lester Adams, don't know him." His voice trailed off, but his lips kept moving. Finally he laid the sheet on the desk and sat back in my swivel-shrieker and took a drink, looking at me for the first time. "It isn't quite up to date. Couple of those guys are pulling hard time. Two are dead, and one might as well be, he's got more tubes sticking out of him than a subway terminal."

"You know lists. They get old just while you're typing them up." I bought a refill.

"Some smart kid in a uniform brought it while I was waiting for you. I gave him a quarter and he looked like I bit his hand. Who sent it?"

"A friend. You wouldn't know him. He respects locks."

His marblelike face didn't move. He'd heard worse. "This to do with the Eccles burn?"

I said nothing. Drank.

"Yeah, Alderdyce said you could shut up like an oyster. I called him. We had quite a conversation about you. Want to know what else he said?"

"No, I want to know what brings you to my office when everyone else's office who has any brains is closed."

"Your client won't answer her phone. Her office is closed too, but it's been closed all day and her home isn't listed. And you're harder to get hold of than an eel with sunburn. I didn't feel like talking to the girl at your service. She sounds like my aunt that tells fortunes. I got to find out if there was any connection between Eccles and Henry Bliss, Dickerson's old bodyguard."

A little chill chased the whisky-warmth up my spine, like a drop of cold water running uphill. "How come?"

"No reason. Except the Denver Police fished a floater out of the South Platte this morning, with two holes in the back of its skull. We got the Telex two hours ago. The stiff fits Bliss's description down to the scar on his chin."

5

I struck a match, cracking the long silence, and touched the flame to a Winston. Gritch watched me. He said:

"Dunked stiffs surface after three days. That puts him in the river just about the time Dickerson and Cole and their boy Phil noticed him missing."

"Meaning?" I flipped the dead match into the ashtray on the desk and cocked a hip up on one corner, blowing smoke out my nostrils.

"Meaning maybe yesterday's try on Dickerson, if that's what

it was, wasn't a backyard job after all. Meaning maybe the same guy that dusted Bliss dusted Eccles. Meaning that seeing as how the two hits were a thousand miles apart and seeing as how the guy that did it didn't leave tracks either time, he's pro after all."

"Slugs match up?"

He shook his fair head without taking his eyes off my face. "Nothing on that yet. But they won't. Major leaguers never use the same piece twice. What I want to know —"

"You said they didn't take their pieces away with them either."

"What I want to know," he went on, "is how it happens I come here looking to talk to you and your client about Eccles' being a mechanic's job and find a list of mechanics all typed up nice and neat before I'm here five minutes."

"Just touching all the bases," I said. "Like you. You didn't send a flyer to Denver looking for some local nut that doesn't like loud music."

"That's it, huh."

I said it was it. He sipped some more Scotch, made a face, rubbed a spot at the arch of his ribcage, and set the glass down. I never knew a cop that didn't have something wrong with his back or his stomach. He said, "Well, I got to talk to Carol Greene."

"I'll set up a meet. What makes it Bliss and Eccles were connected?"

"Nothing. But if it's Dickerson this guy was after, he's a worse shot than I ever heard of."

"Why make the bodyguards targets?"

"That's what I want to ask the Greene woman." He got up, rubbing the spot. The hound's-tooth overcoat he had on was missing a few teeth. "Set it up. Today. I get off at eight."

"How'd Dickerson do last night?"

He opened the door to the outer office. "Capacity crowd. But he don't have the stuff he had when the wife was a fan. When no one shot at him they left disappointed."

He went out. I listened to the hallway door hiss shut behind him against the pressure of the pneumatic device. Thinking.

6

I finished the cigarette and pulled the telephone over and dialed Carol's number. She answered on the third ring.

"Lieutenant Gritch wants to talk to you," I told her, after the preliminaries. "You're better off seeing him at Headquarters. That way you can leave when you want to."

"I already talked to him once. What is it this time?" Her tone was slurred. I'd forgotten she was an alcoholic. I told her about Bliss. After a pause she said, "Ned never mentioned him. I'd know if they ever did business."

"Tell Gritch that."

"You got anything yet?"

"A shadow of a daydream of an idea. I'll let you know. Take a cab to Dearborn."

Next I got the Denver P.I. on the telephone. He said he was still working on the description I'd given him of Henry Bliss. I told him that was all wrapped up and I'd send him a check. Then I called Barry Stackpole.

"That list all right?" he asked.

"A little out of date, according to the cops. I may not need it. Who's on the entertainment desk today?"

"Jed Dutt. I still get my Teacher's, right?"

"If you switch me over to Dutt I'll even throw in a bottle of tonic water."

"Don't be blasphemous." He put me on hold.

"Dutt," announced a rusty old wheeze thirty seconds later.

"My name's Walker," I said. "I'm investigating the attempt on Billy Dickerson's life yesterday. I have a question for you."

"Shoot."

"Very funny," I said.

"Sorry."

I asked him the question. His answer was the first time I got more than one word out of him. I thanked him and broke the connection. The telephone rang while my hand was still on the receiver. It was the man from the union.

"I'm still working on it," I told him. "No money changed hands today."

He said, "Keep an eye on him. He isn't swallowing it or burying it in the basement. I made some inquiries and found out the house across the street is for rent. Maybe you ought to move in."

"Round-the-clock surveillance costs money."

"Name a figure."

I named one. He said, "Can you move in tomorrow?"

I said that was short notice. He said, "Your retainer buys us that right. Shall I make the rental arrangements?"

"I'll let you know," I said.

I smoked a cigarette, looking at the blonde in the bikini on the calendar on the wall opposite the desk. Then I ground out the stub and made one more call. It took a while. When it was finished I got up and unpegged my hat and coat. Before going out I got the Smith & Wesson out of the top drawer of the desk and checked it for cartridges and snapped the holster onto the back of my belt under my jacket. I hate forcing a case.

7

No cops stopped me on my way into the Royal Tower this time, no one was waiting to frisk me when I stepped off the elevator on the third floor. I felt neglected. I rapped on 306.

"What do you want?"

I grinned at Phil. There was no reflection at all in his flat dark eyes. The automatic pistol was a growth in his fist. "This is for the grown-ups," I said. "Any around?"

"You got a lot of smart mouth."

"That makes one of us."

"Phil, who is it?"

The voice was Martin Cole's. It sounded rushed and breathless.

"That snooper," answered Phil, his eyes still on me.

"Tell him to come back later."

"You heard." The man with the gun smiled without opening his lips, like a cat.

A sudden scuffling noise erupted from inside the room. Someone grunted. A lamp turned over with a thud, slinging lariats of shadow up one wall. Phil turned his head and I chopped downward with the edge of my left hand, striking his wrist at the break. He cursed and the gun dropped from his grip. When he stooped to catch it I brought my right fist scooping up, catching him on the point of the chin and closing his mouth with a loud clop. I stepped back to give him room to fall. He used it.

I got the automatic out from under his unconscious body and stepped over him holding it in my sore right hand. I'd barked the knuckles on his obelisk jaw. It was a wasted entrance. Nobody was paying me any attention.

Billy Dickerson, naked but for a pair of blue jockey shorts with his pale belly hanging over the top, was on his knees on the floor astraddle a scarcely more dapper-looking Martin Cole. The manager's tailored jacket was torn and his neatly styled hair hung cockeyed over his left ear. It was the first I knew he wore a wig. Dickerson was holding a shiny steel straight-razor a foot from Cole's throat and Cole had both hands on the singer's wrist trying to keep it there. Dickerson's eyes bulged and his lips were skinned back from long white teeth in a depraved rictus. His breath whistled. Through his own teeth Cole said, "Phil, give me a hand."

Phil wasn't listening. I took two steps forward and swept the butt of the automatic across the base of Dickerson's skull. The singer whimpered and sagged. Falling, the edge of the razor nicked Cole's cheek. It bled.

A floor lamp had been toppled against a chair. I straightened it and adjusted the shade.

"Most people watch television this time of the evening," I said.

The manager paused in the midst of pushing himself free to look at me. Automatically a hand went up and righted his wig. Then he finished rolling the singer's body off his and got up on his knees, listening with head cocked. A drop of blood landed on Dickerson's naked chest with a plop. The manager sat back on his heels. "He's breathing. You hit him damn hard."

"Pistol-whipping isn't an exact science. What happened?"

"D.T.'s. Bad trip. Maybe a combination of the two. He usually doesn't get this violent. When he does, Phil's usually there to get a grip on him and tie him up till it's over." He glanced toward the man lying in the open doorway. "Jeez, what'd you do, kill him?"

"It'd take more than an uppercut to do that. How long's he been like this?"

"Who, Billy? Couple of years. The last few months, though, he's been getting worse. The drugs pump him up for his performances, the booze brings him back down afterwards. But lately it's been affecting his music."

"Not just lately," I said. "It's been doing that for the past year anyway. That's how long attendance at his concerts has been falling off, according to the entertainment writer I spoke to at the *News*."

He had picked up his tinted eyeglasses from the floor and was polishing them with a clean corner of the silk handkerchief he had been using to staunch the trickle of blood from his cut cheek. He stopped polishing and put them on. "Your friend's mistaken. We're sold out."

"They came to see if history would repeat itself and someone would make a new try on Dickerson. Just as you hoped they would."

"Explain."

"First get your hands away from your body."

He smiled. The expression reminded me of Phil's cat's-grin. "If I were armed, do you think I'd have wrestled Billy for that razor barehanded?"

"You would have. He's too valuable to kill. Get 'em up."

He raised his hands to shoulder level. I unholstered my .38 and put the nine-millimeter in my topcoat pocket. Go with the weapon you know.

"There was no hit man," I said, "no attempt on your boy's life. The man you intended to get killed got killed. It was going to be Henry Bliss, but in Denver something went wrong and you had to dump him without trumpets. What did he do, find out what you had planned for him and threaten to go to the law?"

He was still smiling. "You're out of it, Walker. If there was no hit man, who killed Ned Eccles?"

"I'm coming to that. You've got a lot of money tied up in Dickerson, but he's depreciating property. I'm guessing, but I'd say a man with your expensive tastes has a lot of debts, maybe to some people it's not advisable to have a lot of debts with. So you figured to squeeze one more good season out of your client and get out from under. Attempted assassination is box office. A body gives it that authentic touch. After disposing of Bliss you shopped around. I looked pretty good. Security isn't my specialty, my reflexes might not be embarrassingly fast. Also I'm single, with no attachments, no one to demand too thorough an investigation into my death. But I turned you down. Ned Eccles wasn't as good. He was married. But his marriage was sour — you'd have found that out through questioning, as keeping secrets was not one of Ned's specialties — and being an experienced shield he'd have been looking for trouble from outside, not from his employers.

"I called Art Cradshaw a little while ago. That was a mistake, Cole, saying he recommended me. He wasted some of my time being evasive, but when he found out I wasn't dunning him for what he owes me he was willing to talk. He remembered especially how pleased you were to learn I have no family."

Dickerson stirred and groaned. His manager ignored him. Cole wasn't smiling now. I went on.

"What'd you do, promise to cut Phil in on the increased revenue, or just pay him a flat fee to ventilate the bodyguard?"

"Now I know you're out of it. If Phil shot him, where's the gun? His is a nine-millimeter. Eccles was shot with a thirty-eight."

"You were right in front of the service elevator. One of you stepped inside and ditched it. Probably Phil, who was more reliable than Dickerson and tall enough to push open one of the panels on top of the car and stash it there. The cops had no reason to look there, because they were after a phantom hit man who made his escape through the back door."

"You're just talking, Walker. None of it's any good."

"The gun is," I said. "I think you have it hidden somewhere in this suite. The cops will find it. They've been sticking too close to you since the shooting for you to have had a chance to get rid of it. Until now, that is. Where are they?"

"I pulled them off."

The voice was new. I jumped and swung around, bringing the gun with me. I was pointing it at Lieutenant Gritch. He was holding his own service revolver at hip level. Phil lay quietly as ever on the floor between us.

"Put it away," Gritch said patiently. "I don't want to add threatening a police officer to the charge of interfering in an official investigation. Too much paperwork."

I leathered the Smith & Wesson. "You pulled them off why?"

"To give Cole and Scabarda here breathing space. I didn't have enough to get a warrant to search the suite. I had a plainclothes detail in the lobby and near the back entrance ready to follow them until they tried to ditch the piece. Imagine my surprise when one of my men called in to say he saw you going up to the third floor."

"You knew?"

He said, "I'm a detective. You private guys forget that

sometimes. I had to think who stood the most to gain from two dead bodyguards. What tipped you?"

"Cole's story of what happened downstairs. Ned Eccles wouldn't have stopped a bullet meant for his mother. But it didn't mean anything until you said what you did in my office about Dickerson's fans paying to see him get killed."

"Yeah, that's when it hit me too."

"Couple of Sherlocks," I said.

And then the muzzle of Gritch's revolver flamed and the report shook the room and if there had been a mirror handy I'd have seen my hair turn white in that instant. The wind of his bullet plucked at my coat. Someone grunted and I turned again and looked at Cole kneeling on the floor, gripping his bloody right wrist in his left hand. A small automatic gleamed on the carpet between him and Billy Dickerson, the King of Country Rock.

"Circus shooting," Gritch said, disgusted. "If my captain asks, I was aiming for the chest. I got suspended once for getting fancy. Oh, your client's waiting out in the parking lot, shamus. I was questioning her when the call came in. Couldn't talk her out of going. Three sheets to the wind she's still one tough broad. You better see her before she comes up here."

"Yeah," I agreed. "She might kick Cole's head in."

"Guess I'll be able to get that warrant now. You going to be handy for a statement?"

I wrote the address of the shop steward's house in Redford Township on the back of a card and gave it to him. "Don't try to reach me there. I'll be staying in the place across the street for a while starting tomorrow."

"How long?"

"Indefinitely."

"I got a sister-in-law trying to get out of Redford," he said. "I feel sorry for you."

"Like hell you do."

He grinned for the first time since I knew him.

The Prettiest
Dead Girl
in Detroit

1

No one sat in the lobby of the Hotel Woodward anymore. The ceiling was too high, the brass balls on the banister posts were too big, the oak paneling on the walls was carved too deep. The dark red crushed-leather chairs and sofa ached to wrap themselves around someone's thighs, and when I stepped through the front door and closed it against an icy gust the potted fern that occupied the spot on the Persian rug where Theodore Roosevelt had stood to register stirred its dusty fronds like an old man raising his face to the sun. In six months it was all coming down to make room for a ladies' gym.

A geezer with a white moustache growing straight out of his nostrils moved his lips over my ID on the front desk and directed me to Room 212. I climbed a staircase broad enough to roll a rajah's dead elephant down and paused outside an open door with cigarette smoke curling through it. The girl lying on the floor was looking straight at me, but she didn't invite me in. She had learned her lesson the last time. She was a redhead, which I don't guess means much of anything these days, but the red was natural and would look blond in some lights. She had a tan the shade of good brandy covering her evenly from hairline to pink-polished toenails without a bikini line anywhere. It was the only thing covering her. Her body was slim and sleekly muscled, a runner's body. Her eyes were open and very blue. The dark bruises on her throat where the killer's thumbs had gone were the only blemishes I could see.

The investigation business was the same as ever. All the beautiful women I meet are either married or guilty or dead.

There were three men in the room with her, not dead. One was tall and 50 with crisp gray hair to match his suit and very black features carved along the coarse noble lines of a Masai warrior chief. Standing next to him, almost touching him, was a smaller man, fifteen years younger, with dark hair fluffed out on the sides to draw your eyes down from his thinning top to a handlebar moustache someone else trimmed for him and one of those outfits you grin at in magazine ads — plaid jacket over red vest over diamond-patterned sweater over shirt over pink silk scarf with red cherries on it. He looked very white next to the other man. The third man, also white, was very broad across the shoulders, bought his suit in Sears, and combed his hair with a rake. His age had leveled off somewhere between the others'. Guess which one of these men is the hotel dick.

He spotted me first and walked around the body, transferring his cigarette to his lips to take my hand. He had a grip like a rusted bolt. "Amos Walker? Trillen, security officer. I'm the one who called you."

"What seems to be the problem?"

He started a little and looked at me closely. He had gray eyes with all the depth of cigarette foil. "Yeah, I heard you were a comic. The night man, Applegate, gave me your name. You helped him clear up an employee matter a few months back before it got to the papers."

I remembered the case. One of the hops had been letting himself into rooms with a passkey and taking pictures of people who would rather not have had their pictures taken together in hotel rooms. One night he went into 618 looking to Allen-Funt a city councilman with his male aide and got me.

"This is Charles Lemler," Trillen said. "He's with the mayor's press corps. I'll let him tell it."

"Everyone calls me Chuck. Amos, right?" The moustached

man in the noisy outfit grasped the hand Trillen had finished with. Afterward I left it out to dry. "The woman was here when we checked in, just as you see her. The clerk offered to move Mr. De Wolfe to another room before the police got here, but it's going to get out anyway that he registered the day a dead body turned up in the hotel. Trillen suggested you by way of putting some kind of face on this before we call in the authorities."

"Mr. De Wolfe?"

"I'm sorry. Clinton De Wolfe, Amos Walker."

The tall black man standing with his back to the body inclined his head a tenth of an inch in my direction. Well, I'd had my hand wrung enough for one morning.

"Mr. De Wolfe is a former Chicago bank officer," Chuck Lemler explained. "He's the mayor's choice for city controller here."

"Ah."

" 'Ah' means what?" snapped De Wolfe.

"That my mouth is too big for my brain. Sorry. Can I look at the body?"

They made room for me. I checked the face and forehead for bruises and the hair for clotting, found nothing like that, spread my fingers to measure the marks on her neck. The spread was normal and while the dark spots were bigger than my thumbtips they weren't the work of an escaped orangutan or Bigfoot. It takes less strength to strangle a healthy woman than you might think. There was some darkening along her left thigh and under her fingernails. I did a couple of ungallant things with the body and then stood up. My hands felt colder for the contact with her skin. "Cover her."

"You don't like 'em boned?" asked Trillen.

"Trillen, for God's sake!" Lemler's moustache twisted.

"Yeah, yeah." The dick strolled into another room and came back carrying a hotel bedspread under one arm. I took an end and we covered the body. I asked if anyone knew her.

Trillen shook his shaggy head and squashed out his butt in a glass ashtray atop the television set. Well, he'd hear about that from someone. "Just another night rental. I hustle 'em out the back door and they come in again through the side and prowl the bar for fresh meat. This one's new."

"This isn't just another fifty-a-pop career girl," I said. "It takes income to maintain an all-over tan in Michigan in November and the body stinks exclusive health club. Also she didn't die here, or if she did someone moved her. She was lying on that thigh until not too long ago."

"I'd heard politics were rotten in this town," said De Wolfe.

"That's just the sort of knee-jerk assumption we've been fighting for years," Lemler snapped. To me: "There's some opposition to Mr. De Wolfe's choice as controller. But they wouldn't go this far."

"You mean trash a hooker and stash the body in his suite to stir up bad press. It's been done." I shook a Winston out of my pack but stopped short of lighting it. Why later. "My consulting fee's two-fifty, same as my day rate." Lemler nodded. I said, "There's a lieutenant in Homicide named Alderdyce. If you ask him to sit on it he'll do it till it sprouts feathers. But only if you ask him."

De Wolfe glared. "That's your professional advice? Call the police?"

"Not the police. John Alderdyce."

"It's the same thing."

"I just got through telling you it isn't."

Lemler said, "We'll think about it."

I said, "You'll do it. Or I will. Maybe this is common practice at the City-County Building, but on Woodward Avenue it's failure to report a homicide. I have a license to stand in front of."

Trillen said, "Tell him to keep the name of the hotel out of it too."

"That's for the newspapers to decide when it breaks. And

whether you advertise with them heavily enough to make it worth deciding."

"Will you stay on the case regardless?" Lemler asked. "The sooner this gets squared away the better for us, but we can't throw the city's weight behind an ordinary homicide investigation without drawing flies."

"I'll stay as long as the two-fifty holds out. Or until Alderdyce orders me off it," I added.

Lemler produced a checkbook from an inside pocket and began writing. "Will a thousand buy a week of your services?"

"Four days. Not counting expenses."

"The mayor will howl."

"Tell him to make his new raise retroactive to August instead of July."

Trillen called the number I gave him for Alderdyce from downstairs. I was smoking my cigarette in the hall outside when they came, the lieutenant towing a black photographer with a beard like a shotgun pattern and a pale lab man with a shrinking hairline and a young Oriental carrying a black metal case. Alderdyce stopped in front of me. He's my generation, built heavy from the waist up, with facial features hacked out of a charred tree stump blindfolded.

"You didn't burn any tobacco in there?" he demanded. I shook my head. "Thank Christ for small miracles." The group swept in past me. I killed my stub in a steel wall caddy and brought up the rear.

Chuck Lemler broke off a conversation with Clinton De Wolfe to greet the newcomers. But Trillen intercepted Alderdyce and their clasped hands quivered grip for grip until the hotel dick surrendered. Alderdyce wasn't even looking at him. "The body was covered like that when it was found?" Trillen said no. The lieutenant barked at the lab man to take some fiber samples from the blanket and subtract them from whatever else was found on the corpse. He lifted one corner of the blanket.

"Damn."

"Jesus," said the photographer, and took a picture.

I said, "Yeah."

Alderdyce flipped aside the blanket. "Bag her hands," he told the lab man. "There's matter under her fingernails."

"Blood and skin," I said. "She branded somebody."

He looked at me. "I guess you better feed me all of it."

"Strangulation maybe," said the young Oriental, before I could speak. He was down on one knee beside the body with his case open on the floor, prying one of the dead eyelids farther open with a thumb in a surgical glove. "Maybe OD. I'll say what when I get her open."

"No tracks," said Alderdyce, glancing at her wrists and legs.

I said, "There's scar tissue between her toes. I checked."

"Damn nice of you to think to call us in, Walker."

I let that one drift.

"Get some Polaroids," Alderdyce told the photographer. "Last time the shots were three days coming back from the lab." He stopped looking at the body and pointed at the used ashtray. "Careful with that butt. The girl's wearing lipstick. It isn't."

"Uh, that's mine," said Trillen.

The lieutenant swore.

The rest was routine. Under questioning Trillen revealed that the suite had been cleaned the afternoon before and that no one had been inside between then and when the body was found. There were enough passkeys floating around and keys that had gone off with former guests to spoil that angle, and while Lemler maintained that De Wolfe's arrival and the number of his suite had been kept confidential, Trillen admitted that there was no standing on the staff grapevine. Meanwhile the lab man quartered the carpet for stray paperclips, and the photographer, having traded the camera he'd been using for another strung around his neck, took more pictures of the body and laid them on the telephone stand to finish developing. I palmed a good one and let myself out while Alderdyce was politely grilling De Wolfe.

2

Barry Stackpole came out of the YMCA showers scrubbing his sandy hair with a towel, hesitated when he saw me by the lockers, then grinned and lowered the towel to cover his lower body modestly. Only it wasn't his nakedness that embarrassed him, just his Dutch leg. I said, "Doesn't that warp or something?"

He shook his head, reaching for his pants. "Fiberglas. I could've used you out on that handball court a few minutes ago."

"No, you couldn't. I was watching you."

I've known Barry since we shared a shell crater in Cambodia, years before he started his column on organized crime for the Detroit *News* and got his leg and two fingers blown off for his syntax. Someone at the paper had told me I'd find him creaming a Mob attorney on the courts. I held the Polaroid I'd swiped in front of his face while he was tying his shoes. He whistled. "Actress?"

"Prostitute," I said. "Maybe. Know her?"

"Not on my salary. Who squiffed her?"

"Why I'm here. Can you float it among your friends on the well-known Street, put a name to the face? It wouldn't have stayed so pretty very long if she wasn't connected."

He finished drawing on his shirt and put the picture in the breast pocket. "User?"

"Yeah. Either someone throttled her unconscious and then shot too much stuff to her or shot too much stuff to her and couldn't wait. While you're at it, feed Clinton De Wolfe to your personal computer and see what it belches out."

"I know that name."

"If you do you heard it from your guy on city government. He'll be fine-tuning the books if the mayor gets his way."

"That isn't it. When I remember what it was I'll get back to you." He took down a bottle of mouthwash from the shelf in his locker and unscrewed the cap. "How rich does this little errand stand to make me?"

"A century, if I like what I hear. Otherwise seventy-five."

"Century either way. Plus a fifth of Jack Daniel's."

"I thought you were on the wagon."

"It's a cold dry ride." He hoisted the mouthwash. "Cold steel."

"Hot lead," I returned. The joke toast was as old as the last Tet offensive and the stuff in the bottle smelled like rye. I left him.

3

My office waiting room was full of no customers. I unlocked the door to the brain trust, forward-passed a sheaf of advertising circulars I found under the mail slot to the wastebasket, pegged my hat and coat, and set the swivel behind the desk to squeaking while I broke the Scotch out of the deep drawer. There was frost on the window, frost on my soul. I guessed Barry had found my breath sweet enough not to need help. As the warmth crawled through my veins I dialed my service. John Alderdyce had tried to reach me twice. I knew why. I asked the girl to hold any further calls from him and thumbed down the plunger and tried another number from memory. A West Indies accent answered on the third ring, cool and female.

"Iris, this is Amos."

"Amos who?"

"It's a funny hooker," I said dryly. "I'm trying to identify a lady who might have been in your line. Five-six and a hundred and ten, red and blue, Miami tan, about thirty. She showed up dead in a suite in the Woodward this morning. Drugs and strangulation. She wasn't a stranger to the drugs."

"Sounds a little rich for the street."

"You get around."

"In Blacktown. You're talking Grosse Pointe chic. Try the escort services."

"The real ones or the fronts?"

"There's a difference?"

"That's all you can tell me, huh."

"Every one of us don't know everyone else," she retorted, her class slipping. "Amos?"

I'd started to peg the receiver. I raised it again and said yeah. After a pause she said, "I'm going home."

"Home where?"

"Home where. Home the island. I'm going back to live with my mother."

"I'm glad," I said after a moment. "It's what you've been wanting."

"That's all? I thought maybe you'd try to talk me out of it."

"I don't have any hold on you, Iris."

"No. I guess you don't."

"Have a good flight." I was speaking into a dead line.

I looked at the calendar on the wall across from my framed investigator's license. Then I looked at a pigeon shivering alone on the ledge of the apartment house facing my building. Then I looked at the calendar again to see what the date was. I winched the Yellow Pages out of the top drawer and looked up Escorts.

I tried the display advertisements first and got three possibles. Then I tried the cheaper listings and lucked out on the first call.

"I need an escort for a business party Friday night," I told the woman who answered, by rote. "What I'm interested in is a specific redhead I saw with a friend of mine in the restaurant of the Hotel Woodward recently. I didn't get her name but I think she's with your service." I described her.

"That sounds like Myra Langan," said the woman. "But she doesn't work here anymore."

"Did she resign?"

"I'm not at liberty to say."

"That means she was fired."

"I'm not —"

"Can I talk to you about her in person? It's important."

"We have another redhead," she started to say. I told her I'd pay for her time. She hesitated, then said, "Our regular escort fee is a hundred dollars." I said that sounded fair and agreed to meet her in the office at three. "Ask for Linda."

It was just past noon. I thought about the woman's voice. She sounded pleasant and young. You can't always get the accent you want. I skipped lunch and drove to a downtown theater where an old Robert Mitchum detective film was playing in revival. I took notes. In the lobby afterward I used the pay telephone to call Barry Stackpole's private number at the *News*.

"Nobody I showed the picture to knows her from Jane Fonda," he told me. "Could be I'm working the wrong level. All the *capos* are browning their bellies at Cannes this time of year."

"Try Myra Langan. I've got an appointment today with a woman she worked with at a legit floss rental firm." I named the place.

"Our guy on cophouse might turn something. It means bringing him in."

"Cut the best deal you can." I took the instrument away from my ear.

"Don't you want to hear what I found out about Clinton De Wolfe?"

I paused. "I'm on pins and noodles."

"I get an exclusive when this breaks, right?"

"Feed it to me."

"I finally remembered where I'd heard the name and hooked a snitch," he said. "De Wolfe is on the books as having resigned his vice-presidency at a Chicago bank in September. The dope is he was forced out for making unsecured loans to a Mob subsidiary in Evanston and accepting repayment in cash skimmed from the tables in Vegas."

I looked at a stiff face reflected in the telephone's shiny steel cradle. "Laundering?"

"Yeah. They let him quit to duck bad press. Good?"

"Listen, I'm on my way to your office with a C-note and a fifth of JD. Have that picture ready, okay?"

"Bring a glass for yourself." He broke the connection.

4

It was a quick stop and a quicker drink. From there I drove downriver to a low yellow brick building between a beauty salon and a hairpiece emporium with the escort firm's name etched in elegant script across the front. Inside was an office decorated like a living room with a white shag rug and ivory curtains and a lot of blond furniture, including a tall occasional table with turned legs and a glass top, but it didn't fool me, I know a desk when I see one. A brunette with her hair piled atop her head in blue waves and the kind of cheeks girls used to have their back teeth hauled out to get sat behind it wearing a black dress with a scoop neck and pearl buttons in her ears. I took off my hat and asked for Linda.

"You're Mr. Walker?" I said I was. "I'm Linda."

I glanced around. The room took up the entire ground floor and we were the only ones in it. "Who was I supposed to ask?"

"I wanted to get a look at you. In this business we have to go out with whoever has the price and no bloodstains on his necktie. When I get the chance to choose I leap on it. Are you a daylighter or a sundowner?" I must have looked as stupid as I felt, because she said, "A sundowner waits for darkness before he'll take a drink. It's dark in England."

"My father's family was English."

She smiled and rose. "I'll get my coat and purse."

We went to a place down the street with a blue neon cocktail glass on the roof and took a booth upholstered in red vinyl around a table the size of a hubcap. She ordered something green. I took Scotch and when the waitress left I slid the Polaroid shot I had gotten back from Barry across the table. Linda's nostrils whitened when she glanced down at it. Then she looked at me.

"You're not a policeman. Your eyes are too gentle."

"I'm a private investigator." I tapped the picture. "Myra Langan?"

"It's her. Are you looking for her murderer?"

"Who said murder?"

"She was the kind of a girl who would wind up murdered or suicided. Did she kill herself?"

"Not unless she found a way to strangle herself barehanded. What kind of a girl is the kind that would wind up murdered or suicided?"

She sipped her drink and set it down. After a beat I passed her two fifties. With what I'd given Barry, that left me just fifty from the first day of my retainer. I was on the wrong end of the information business.

"Myra got fired for her action on the side," said Linda, snapping shut her purse. "The police keep a tight eye on the escort business for just that. It was can her or risk a raid."

"Who snitched on her?"

"Another girl, Susan. They were at the same party and Susan overheard Myra discussing terms with her escort. Myra tried to cut her in but she wasn't having any."

"Myra got canned on just her word?"

"The boss lady ran a check. Her brother's a retired cop. He interviewed some of Myra's regular customers. The same pimp put six of them on her scent."

"What'd he interview them with, a Louisville Slugger?"

"He's retired like I said." She licked a drop off the end of her swizzle stick, eyeing me. "Married?"

"Not recently. Was she using when she worked for the firm?"

"You mean drugs? She couldn't have been. A complete physical is part of the screening process for new employees."

"Could've happened after she was hired. She worked there how long?"

"She was there when I came. A year, maybe. You think the pimp turned her on to get a handle on her?"

"It's not new. Looks like hers run high in executive circles. He have a name?"

"Probably. Talk to Max Montemarano. That's the boss lady's brother. He's a day guard at Detroit Bank and Trust. The main branch."

I got up and left money on the table for the drinks. "Thanks. I have to see a man."

"Me, too." She swung a mile of silk-paved leg out from under the table. "What do you do when you're not detecting?"

I watched her stand up. Some women know how to get out of a booth. I asked her if she'd ever lived on an island.

"What? No."

"Okay, thanks again."

On my way out a man in a blue suit seated near the door looked from me to the woman in the black dress standing by the booth and then back to me. I agreed with him.

5

I called the bank from an open-air booth outside a service station. A receptionist got me Montemarano, who explained in a hard fat man's voice that his shift didn't change for another hour but agreed to stop by my office on his way home for a quick fifty. The expenses on this one had just caught up with my fee.

A kid in a plaid overcoat stood in the foyer of my building reading the sign on the building super's door. The sign read MANAGER. He was still studying when I reached the second-floor landing. He might as well have worn a uniform.

I found Lieutenant John Alderdyce sitting on the bench in my waiting room learning about the Man of some other Year from a copy of *Time* he'd unstuck from the coffee table. He had on a tan jacket and a red knit tie over a champagne-colored shirt. Since I knew him he'd dressed from nowhere closer to the street than J. L. Hudson's second floor. "This year it's a computer," he said, flicking his fingers at the photograph on the cover. "What do you think about a machine making the cover of *Time?*"

"Electricity's cheap. You and I run on tobacco and alcohol." I unlocked the inner office door. "Someone should enroll your boy in the lobby in a remedial reading course."

"He's on loan from the commissioner's office. His Police Positive has an ivory handle." He got up and followed me inside, where I shed my outerwear and sat down and got an old bill from under the desk blotter and pretended to check the arithmetic. He thumped his hand down on the desk, palm up. "The photog used up a twelve-pack of Polaroid film at the Woodward. He wound up with eleven pictures."

I started to reach for my inside breast pocket, then remembered I'd left the picture of Myra Langan on the table where I'd had drinks with Linda. "I'll stand the department to a new pack tomorrow."

"You wouldn't be prowling around in an open homicide investigation," he said. "Not you."

"It happens we're both working for the city this one time. Check with Lemler."

"No thanks. Every time I look at that guy's clothes and shut my eyes I see spots. What'd you turn?"

I watched him. He had sad eyes. Cops do, and it doesn't mean anything more than a croc's smile. Finally I said, "Her name was Myra Langan. She worked for an escort service downtown till they booted her for soliciting." I told him which service and gave him Linda's name. I didn't mention Max Montemarano or the pimp. It weighed light without them and Alderdyce saw it. He said, "I guess you stopped here on your way to Headquarters."

"More or less."

"More less than more. You passed Headquarters on your way here."

"I wanted to see if I had customers."

"No good. Go again."

"I'm a small guy in a small business, John. I don't have your resources."

"Resources. The redhead — Myra? — rode the springs with some guy not long before she was killed, the M.E. said. He took a smear and the type matches the blood we found under her fingernails. She was alive until four this morning. I've got men knocking on doors in the hotel looking for busted lamps and shaving cuts that don't fit a razor and scouting up the night staff, which by now is scattered between here and Ann Arbor. It's a big hotel, Walker. It has a big staff and lots of rooms. If I could put the squad on it I'd have the answers I need in an hour. But police reporters notice when the squad's missing and start asking questions. I've got Junior downstairs and one other detective and two uniforms borrowed from Traffic. I can't even get priority at the lab because someone who knows the number of one of this town's three TV stations might be looking."

He stuck his brutal face inches from mine. "Those are my resources, Walker. Four men, and the mayor's dresser asking me every five minutes when I'm going to arrest someone.

You're a detective. Does it look to a detective like I need a keyholer playing Go Fish with me too?"

"I'm waiting to hear it," I said.

"Hear what?"

" 'Get off my foot or I'll jerk your license.' "

Alderdyce lifted weights when he wasn't sifting leads. He gave the desk a shove and it struck me in the solar plexus and I rolled backward on squealing casters and came to a rest pinned against the window. He leaned on the desk.

"We've never mixed it up, you and me," he said. "You'd lose."

We stayed like that for a long moment, he resting his weight on the desk, I trying to breathe with the edge pressing my sternum and cold from the window glass soaking clammily through my jacket and shirt to my back. Then he pushed off and turned around and left. The door drifted shut against the pressure of the pneumatic closer.

John and I had played together as kids, a million years ago.

Max Montemarano found me straightening the furniture in the office a few minutes later. He wasn't fat at all, just large and slope-shouldered with a civilian overcoat over his gray guard's uniform and a visored cap on the back of his white head. His face was broad and ruddy, and burst blood vessels etched purple tributaries on his cheeks. "Colder'n a witch's tit," he said by way of greeting.

I blew dust out of a pair of pony glasses and filled them with Scotch. He managed to snatch one up without spilling anything, lifted it in a sort of toast, and knocked it back the way they used to do in westerns. When the glass came down empty I poked a fifty-dollar bill into it. "Myra Langan," I said.

He looked down at the bill without touching it. "What about her?"

"You followed up another girl's complaint about her for your sister. She had a pimp. He had a name."

He set the glass down on the desk and drew himself up, squaring his visor. "I'm not a cop anymore. She ain't working for my sister now. I never dipped a finger in twenty-three years on the force and I ain't about to start now."

I said, "She's dead. There's a better than even chance her pimp killed her or knows who did."

He hesitated. I uncapped the bottle again and moved it toward his glass. He scooped out the bill and straightened it between his fingers and folded it and put it in his breast pocket and snapped the flap shut. I poured. He put down half.

"He was a regular customer of Myra's until he stopped coming in," he said. "That was about the time the first John was approached." A brow got knitted. "Wilson. Jim Wilson."

"Fat, short, tall, skinny, black, white, what?"

"White. Not fat. Thick like me. He had the widest shoulders for his height of any man I ever seen. Wider than yours. Wore cheap suits."

I was lighting a Winston. I avoided burning any fingers putting out the flame. "Shaggy head? A smoker?"

"Like a stack at the River Rouge plant. And if the guy combed his hair at all —"

I came around the desk and armed him toward the door. "Thanks for coming in."

"My drink."

I handed him the glass and the bottle and held the door. "Happy Thanksgiving."

After the outer door closed on Montemarano I made a call and then unlocked the top drawer of the desk, checked my Smith & Wesson for cartridges, and clipped the holster to my belt under the tail of my jacket. It was heavier than a rabbit's foot but felt just as good.

6

The same geezer was sorting mail into the pigeonholes behind the desk at the Woodward when I strode past heading for the stairs. The letters might have come Pony Express. I knocked at

212 and Trillen opened the door. The hotel dick was alone in the suite with a chalk outline on the carpet where the dead girl had been lying. I asked him where Chuck Lemler and Clinton De Wolfe were.

"Coming. De Wolfe changed hotels. What's it about?"

I walked around, poking my head into the other rooms. The air smelled of cigarettes and there were three butts in the ashtray on the television set, all Trillen's brand. He'd been waiting there since taking my call. "Applegate offered me a job nightside," I said. "The pay stunk. Head of security pay any better?"

"Not much. It ain't open anyway."

"Not yet."

De Wolfe and Lemler arrived fifteen minutes later. The black controller-to-be looked tall and gaunt in a dark overcoat and gray scarf. Lemler had on a horse blanket and one black glove and the other in his fist posing as a riding crop. "I hope you have something," Lemler demanded. "The mayor wants to avoid identifying Mr. De Wolfe with this hotel any more than is absolutely necessary."

"I agree. It's bad enough he's identified with his old bank."

De Wolfe measured me out some of his icy glare.

I said, "You took early retirement. The board of directors was all for it. If the stockholders found out you'd been using bank funds to launder Mob money they'd clear the executive offices."

"You're drunk!" Lemler was paler than usual.

"It was a frame," said De Wolfe. "A good vice-president makes enemies. It was the only way they could get rid of me."

"It's probably true or you would've let it go to court," I said. "But it rules out the theory that your opponents here dumped a body in your suite to embarrass you. They have access to my information; the publicity from that Mob tie-in alone would have been enough to take you out of the running for city office. They didn't have to commit murder too." I turned to

Lemler. "Chuck, I owe you five hundred from the retainer you gave me. I spent two-fifty. I'll eat the price of the whisky."

"I didn't pay you to fork up dirt on my employer's choice for controller." He was twisting his glove.

"No, you paid me to find out who killed Myra Langan. That was the name of the murdered girl.

"Someone thought she was too pretty to throw away on old men at dinner parties in Birmingham and Grosse Pointe," I went on. "This someone started seeing her as a customer of the escort service she worked for and when he had her confidence he hooked her on drugs to make her easier to steer. He was in a line of work that put him in contact with useful people on every level. When it came time to collect for the stuff he was supplying her, he put her to work. Some men would pay two hundred dollars for twenty minutes with a girl like Myra. For a time it was sweet. But one night something tilted, as things will in business relationships of that nature, and she became a liability. As her pimp he was used to favors other than money; he picked an intimate moment to strangle her senseless and then load her with enough dope to send her over. It would look like accidental death or suicide. Only he hadn't counted on her throat showing the bruises his fingers made after death. He'd forgotten how strong his hands were."

It was warm in the room, but none of us who were wearing overcoats had moved to take his off. Trillen, wearing the same baggy gray suit I had met him in, hadn't stirred at all. I put my hands in the pockets of my coat and said, "But pimps are nothing if not resourceful. It happened that a political big gun was stopping at the hotel later that morning. If her body were found in his suite it would change the whole complexion of the investigation. This particular pimp had access to the service elevator and the authority to see to it that all the employees that might be prowling the halls at four in the morning were in another part of the hotel when he moved the corpse. The bare chance that a stray guest might spot him was worth taking.

Bringing in a P.I. later to muck things up worse didn't hurt.

"How's the back, Wilson?" I asked Trillen. "You ought to get iodine on those scratches before they infect."

The hotel dick's mouth smiled. "You're just stirring ashes. No proof."

"Applegate, the night man, will remember you were in the hotel this morning hours before your shift started. Whatever excuse you made won't stand. You're wearing Myra's marks and I spoke to a man today who will identify you as her pimp. Take a fellow sleuth's advice and plead guilty to second-degree. The city will want to get this one under glass in a hurry. Am I right, Chuck?"

"I'll advise the mayor," said Lemler. He and De Wolfe were staring at Trillen, who was moving his huge shoulders around under his jacket. The dick said:

"I didn't hook her. She was shooting between her toes when I met her. Whatever croaker gave her the nod at the escort place wasn't thorough. It was business all the way with us; I got her the stuff, she wiggled her tail at conventions and some-times for me."

"What was she doing, moonlighting on you?" I asked.

"That wouldn't have been so bad, but she started doing it here where I work. I like this job and I busted my butt to get it. I left something here last night and when I came in for it I found her working the bar. She tried to sugar me out of my mad in one-ten. I went crazy in the middle of it. I thought she was dead. I OD'd her to make it look like an accident, but then the bruises started to show. Well . . ." He put a hand behind his back as if to stretch and brought it around with a gun in it.

"Let it go."

Trillen swung toward the new voice, bringing the gun with him. John Alderdyce, standing in the open door to the hallway, crouched with his .38 stretched out in front of him in both hands. The hotel man dropped his weapon and threw his palms into the air.

"Okay," called the lieutenant.

The kid in the plaid overcoat entered from the bedroom with his gun drawn. He holstered it, frisked Trillen against a wall, cuffed him, and started droning from a printed card he carried in his shirt pocket.

"Fire escape," explained Alderdyce, tucking away his own gun. "Junior was still in your building when Montemarano came out. We questioned him. I figured you'd come straight here. You should have called me."

"I had to earn my fee first," I said.

"You cut it fine."

"Not so fine." I pulled my right hand out of my coat pocket wrapped around the butt of the Smith & Wesson and returned it to its holster.

We shook hands.

De Wolfe said, "Lieutenant, may I go now? I just have time to book the evening flight back to Chicago."

Lemler was standing by the window with his face on the floor. I went over there. "We didn't know about De Wolfe," he said.

"I believe you. Look on it as a break. The opposition would have run it up the nearest flagpole. Everybody crapped out on this one. The mayor lost an appointee, De Wolfe lost a good job, Trillen's out the next ten to twenty, and Myra Langan's behind one life. She was too pretty to live."

"You're the only one better off than he was this morning," Lemler said.

I looked out the window. My lone pigeon or one like it had followed me there and was perched on the ledge between gimcracks, looking cold and dirty and miserable and like the only pigeon in the whole world.

"Yeah, I'm way ahead."

Blond and Blue

Ernest Krell's aversion to windows was a legend in the investigation business. It was a trademark, like his gunmetal tie clasp made from a piece of shrapnel the army surgeons had pried out of his hip in Seoul and his passion for black suits with discreet patterns to break up their severity. During his seventeen years with the Secret Service he had spent so many public hours warning presidential candidates' wives away from windows that when it came time to open his own detective agency he dug into his wife's inheritance to throw up a building that didn't have any. Narrow vertical slits set eight feet apart let light into a black marble edifice that looked like a blank domino from anywhere along the Detroit River.

A receptionist with blue stones in her ears and that silver complexion that comes free with fluorescent lights took my hat and left me alone in Krell's office, a bowling alley of a room carpeted in black and brown and containing oak-and-leather chairs and an antique desk in front of a huge Miró landscape, lots of blues and reds, to make up for the lack of a window. The walls were painted two shades of cinnamon, darker on the desk side of the office to keep the customers where they belonged. A lot of framed citations, Krell's license, and a square black-on-white sign reading RELIANCE — *"Courtesy, Efficiency, Confidentiality"* took care of the bare spots.

There were no ashtrays, so I took a seat near a potted fern and lit a cigarette, tipping my ashes into the pot. After five puffs the man himself came in through a side door and scowled at the curling smoke and then at me and said, "There's no smoking in this building."

"I didn't see any signs," I said.

"You don't see any ashtrays either." He ran a hand under the edge of the desk. A second later, the silver-skinned receptionist came in carrying an ashtray made just for putting out smokes in and I did that. I couldn't decide if it was the way he had pushed the button or if I just had the look of a guy that would light up in the boss's office. When she left carrying my squashed butt the man extended his hand and I rose to take it. His grip was cool and firm and as personal as a haberdasher's smile.

"Good to meet you, Walker. I don't think I've had the pleasure."

"This is the first time I've gotten any higher than the fourth floor," I said.

Krell chuckled meaninglessly. He was six-three and two hundred, a large pale man with black hair that looked dyed and wrinkles around his eyes and mouth from years of squinting into the sun looking for riflemen on rooftops. It was orange today, orange stripes on his black suit and jaunty orange sunbursts on his silk tie to pick it up. It softened the overall effect of his person like a bright ribbon tied to a buffalo's tail made you forget he was standing on your foot. The famous tie clasp was in place.

He waved me back into my chair but remained upright at parade rest with his hands folded behind him. "I spent last night reading the files on the cases you assisted us with," he said. "Despite the fact that you're anything but the Reliance type" — his gaze lit on my polyester gabardine — "you show a certain efficiency I admire. Also you spend more time and effort on each client than a Reliance operative could afford."

"You can do that when they only come into your office one at a time," I volunteered.

"Yes." He let the word melt on his tongue, then pressed on. "The reason I asked you to come down today, we have a client

who might best benefit from your rather unorthodox method.
A delicate case and a highly emotional one. Frankly, I'd have
referred her to another agency had she not come recommended by one of our most valued clients."

"She?"

"You'll meet her in a moment. It's a missing persons situation, which I believe is your specialty. Her son's been kidnaped."

"That's the FBI's specialty."

"Only in cases where ransom is demanded. On the statutes
it's abduction, which would make it a police matter except that
her ex-husband is the suspected culprit. The authorities consider that a domestic problem and approach it accordingly."

"Meaning it gets spiked along with the butcher's wife who
threw a side of pork at her husband," I said. "How old is the
boy?"

"Seven." He quarter-turned toward the desk and drew a
typewritten sheet from a folder lying open on top. "Blond and
blue, about four feet tall leaning to pudgy, last seen April third
wearing a blue-and-white-striped T-shirt, red corduroy shorts,
and dirty white sneakers. Answers to Tommy. One minute he
was playing with a toy truck in the front yard of his mother's
home in Austin, Texas, and the next there was just the truck.
Neighbor thought he saw him on the passenger's side of a low
red sports car going around the corner. The ex-husband owns
a red Corvette."

"That's April third this year?" I asked. It was now early
May.

"I know it's a long time. She's been to all the authorities
here and in Texas."

"Why here?"

"A relative of the mother's is sure she saw the father at the
Tel-Twelve Mall in Southfield three weeks ago. She flew in
right after. Staying at the relative's place there."

"What makes it too hot to touch?"

He stroked the edge of the sheet with a meaty thumb,

making a noise like a cricket. "The ex-husband is an executive with a finance corporation I sometimes do business with. If it gets out I'm investigating one of its employees —"

"Last stop for the money train," I finished. "What's to investigate? She should've gone back to court to start, put the sheriffs on his neck."

"His neck is gone and so is he. He took a leave of absence from his company, closed out his apartment in Austin, and vanished, boy and all. He probably had all his bags packed in the Corvette's trunk when he picked up Tommy and just kept driving. It's all here." He put the sheet back inside the folder and handed the works to me.

It ran just five pages, triple-spaced and written in Reliance's terse patented preliminary-report language, but on plain paper without the distinctive letterhead. Very little of it was for me. The ex-husband's name was Frank Corcoran. He was a house investments counselor for Great Western Loans and Credit, with branch offices in seventeen cities west of the Mississippi. There were two numbers to call for information there. The name and number of the witness who had seen his car at the time of the boy's disappearance were there too, along with the 'Vette's serial number and license plate. It was long gone by now or the cops in Austin or Detroit would have had it in on a BOL weeks ago. I folded the report into quarters anyway and put it in a pocket and gave back the empty folder. "Can I talk to the mother?"

"Of course. She's in the other office."

I followed him through the side door into a room separate from the one where the receptionist sat, a chamber half the size of Krell's decorated in muted warm colors and containing a row of chairs with circular backs, like the room in a funeral home where the family receives visitors. "Charlotte Corcoran, Amos Walker," said Krell.

The woman seated on the end chair raised a sunken face to look at me. Her jaw was too long to be pretty, but it had been an attractive face before she started losing weight, the bones sculpted, not sharp like now, the forehead high and broad instead of jutting and hollow at the sides. The little bit of lipstick she wore might have been painted on the corpse in that same funeral home. Her hair was blond and tied back loosely with wisps of gray springing loose around her ears. Her dress was just a dress and her bare angular legs ended in bony feet thrust into low-heeled shoes a size too large for her. She was smoking a cigarette with a white filter tip. I peered through the haze at Krell, who moved a shoulder and then flipped a wall switch that started a fan humming somewhere in the woodwork. The smoke stirred and began twisting toward a remote corner of the ceiling. I got out a Winston and sent some of my own after it.

"My boy Tommy turned seven last week," Charlotte Corcoran told the wall across from her. "It's the first birthday I missed."

Her speech had an east Texas twang. I twirled another chair to face hers and sat down. The connecting door clicked shut discreetly behind Krell. It was the only noise he made exiting. "Tell me about your husband," I said.

She snicked some ash into a tray on the chair next to her and looked at me. Seeing me now. "I could call him a monster. I'd be lying. Before this the worst thing he did was to call a half hour before supper to say he was working late. He did that a lot; it's part of why I divorced him. That's old news. I want my son back."

"What'd the police in Austin say?"

"They acted concerned until I told them he'd been kidnaped by his father. Then they lost interest. They said they'd put Tommy's picture on the bulletin board in every precinct, and maybe they did. They didn't give it to the newspapers or TV the way they do when a child's just plain missing. I got the same swirl of no action from the police here. Kidnaping's okay between relatives, I guess." She spat smoke.

"Skipping state lines should've landed it in the feds' lap," I said.

"I called the Houston office of the FBI. They were polite. They test high on polite. They said they'd get it on the wire. I never saw any of them."

"So far as you know."

It was lost on her. She mashed out her butt, leaving some lipstick smeared on the end. "I spent plenty of time at Police Headquarters here and back home," she said. "They showed me the door nice as you please, but they showed me the door. They wouldn't tell me what they'd found out."

"That should have told you right there."

Her expression changed. "Can you find them, Mr. — I've forgotten."

"Walker," I said. "A lot rests on whether they're still here. And if they were ever here to begin with."

"Frank was. My cousin Millie doesn't make mistakes."

"That's Millicent Arnold, the relative you're staying with?" She nodded. "I'll need a picture of Tommy and one of Mr. Corcoran."

"This should do it." From her purse she drew a 5x7 bureau shot and gave it to me. "I took it last summer on a trip to Corpus Christi. Tommy's grown several inches since. But his face hasn't changed."

I looked at a man with dark curly hair and a towheaded boy standing in swim trunks on a yellow beach with blue ocean behind them. "His father didn't get that build lifting telephone receivers."

"He worked out at a gym near his office. He was a member."

I pocketed the photograph next to the Reliance report and stood up. "I'll be in touch."

"I'll be in."

Krell was on the intercom to his receptionist when I reentered his office. I waited until he finished making his lunch reservation, then:

"How much of a boost can I expect from Reliance on this one?"

"You already have it," he said. "The situation is —"

"Delicate, yeah. I'll take my full fee, then. Three days to start."

"What happened to professional courtesy?"

"It went out of style, same as the amateur kind. What about it? You're soaking her five bills per day now."

"Four-fifty." He adjusted his tie clasp. "I'll have Mrs. Marble draw you a check."

"Your receptionist has access to company funds?"

"She's proven herself worthy of my trust."

I didn't say it. My bank balance was stuck to the sidewalk as it was.

2

The report had Mrs. Corcoran in contact with a Sergeant Grandy in General Service, missing persons detail. I deposited half of the Reliance check at my bank, hanging on to the rest for expenses, and drove down to Police Headquarters, where a uniform escorted me to a pasteboard desk with a bald head behind it. Grandy had an egg salad sandwich in one hand and a Styrofoam cup of coffee in the other and was using a blank arrest form for a placemat. He wore a checked sportcoat and a moustache healthy enough to have sucked all the hair from his scalp.

"Corcoran, yeah," he said, after reading my card and hearing my business. "It's in the works. You got to realize it don't get the same priority as a little boy lost. I mean, somebody's feeding him."

"Turn anything yet?"

"We got the boy's picture and the father's description out."

"That's what you've done. What've you got?"

He flicked a piece of egg salad off his lapel. "What I got is two Grosse Pointe runaways to chase down and a four-year-old girl missing from an apartment on Watson I'll be handing to

Homicide soon as she turns up jammed in a culvert somewhere. I don't need part-time heat too."

We were getting started early. I set fire to some tobacco.
"Who's your lieutenant?"

"Winkle. Only he's out sick."

"Sergeant Grandy, if I spent an hour here, would I walk out
any smarter than I was when I came in?"

"Probably not."

"Okay. I just wondered if you were an exception."

I was out of there before he got it.

On the ground floor I used a pay telephone to call the
Federal Building and explained my problem to the woman
who answered at the FBI.

"That would be Special Agent Roseman, Interstate Flight,"
she said. "But he's on another line."

I said I'd wait. She put me on hold. I watched a couple of
prowl-car cops sweating in their winter uniforms by the Coke
machine. After five minutes the woman came back on. "Mr.
Roseman will be tied up for a while. Would you like to call
back?"

I said yeah and hung up. Out on Beaubien the sidewalks
were throwing back the first real heat of spring. I rolled down
the window on the driver's side and breathed auto exhaust all
the way to my office building. You have to celebrate it somehow.

3

The window in my thinking parlor was stuck shut. I strained a
disc heaving it open a crack to smell the sweet sun-spread
pavement three stories down. Then I sat down behind the
desk — real wood, no longer in style but not yet antique —
and tried the FBI again. Roseman was out to lunch. I left my
number and got out the Reliance report and dialed one of the

two numbers for the firm where Frank Corcoran worked in Austin.

"Great Western." Another woman. They own the telephone wires.

I gave her my name and calling. "I'm trying to reach Frank Corcoran. It's about an inheritance."

"I'm sorry, Mr. Corcoran is on indefinite leave."

"Where can I reach him?"

"I'm sorry."

I thanked her anyway and worked the plunger. I wasn't disappointed. It's basic to try the knob before you break out the lock picks. I used the other number, and this time I got a man.

"Arnold Wilson, president of Thornbraugh Electronics in Chicago," I said. Thornbraugh Heating & Cooling put out the advertising calendar tacked to the wall across from my desk. "We're building a new plant in Springfield and Frank Corcoran advised me to call Great Western for financing. Is he in?"

"What did you say your name was?" I repeated it. "One moment."

I had enough time to pluck out a cigarette before he came back on the line. "Are you the private investigator who spoke to my partner's secretary about Mr. Corcoran a few moments ago?" His tone had lost at least three layers of silk.

"What's the matter, you don't have any walls in that place?"

I was talking to myself. As I lowered the dead receiver I could hear the computers gossiping among themselves, trashing my credit rating. The laugh was on them; I didn't have one.

4

My next trip was through the Yellow Pages. There were at least fifty public gymnasiums listed within a half hour of downtown Detroit, including Southfield, any one of which would suit Corcoran's obsession with a healthy body. We all have our white whales. I made a list of the bigger, cleaner places. It was still long. Just thinking about it made my feet throb.

I tried the number of the place where Charlotte Corcoran was staying in Southfield. A breathy female voice answered, not hers.

"Millicent Arnold?"

"Yes. Mr. Walker? Charlotte told me she spoke with you earlier. She's napping now. Shall I wake her?"

"That's okay. It's you I want to talk to. About the man you saw who looked like Frank Corcoran."

"It was Frank. I spent a week in their home in Austin last year and I know what he looks like."

"Where did you see him at the mall? In what store?"

"He was coming out of the sporting goods place. I was across the corridor. I almost called to him over the crowd, but then I remembered. I thought about following him, see where he went, but by the time I made up my mind he was lost in the crush. I went into the store and found the clerk who had waited on him. He'd paid cash for what be bought, didn't leave a name or address."

"What'd he buy, barbell weights?" Maybe he was working out at home and I could forget the gyms.

"No. Something else. Sweats, I think. Yes , a new sweatsuit. Does that help?"

"My feet will give you a different answer. But yeah. Thanks, Miss Arnold."

"Call me Millie. Everyone does."

I believed her. It was the voice.

After saying good-bye I scowled at the list, then raised my little electronic paging device from among the flotsam in the top drawer of the desk and called my answering service to test the batteries. They were deader than the Anthony dollar. I said I'd call in for messages and locked up.

The office directly below mine was being used that month

by a studio photographer, five foot one and three hundred pounds, with a Marlboro butt screwed into the middle of a face full of stubble. I went through the open door just as he finished brushing down the cowlick of a gap-toothed ten-year-old in a white shirt buttoned to the neck and blue jeans as stiff as aluminum siding and waddled around behind the camera, jowls swinging. "Smile, you little —" he said, squeezing the bulb on the last part. White light bleached the boy's face and the sky-blue backdrop behind.

When the kid had gone, following the spots in front of his eyes, I handed the photographer the picture Charlotte Corcoran had given me of her ex-husband and their son. "How much to make a negative from this and run off twenty-five prints?" I asked.

He held the shot close enough to his face to set it afire if his stub were burning. "Eighty-seven fifty."

"How much for just fifteen?"

"Eighty-seven fifty."

"Must be the overhead." I was looking at a rope of cobwebs as thick as my wrist hammocking from the ceiling.

"No, you just look like someone that wants it tomorrow."

"Early." I gave him two fifties and he changed them from a cigar box on a table cluttered with lenses and film tubes and wrote me out a receipt.

I used his telephone to call my service. There were no messages. I tried the Federal Building again. Special Agent Roseman had come in and gone out and wasn't expected back that day. He had the right idea. I went home and cooked a foil-wrapped tray for supper and watched the news and a TV movie and went to bed.

5

I was pulling a tail.

Leaving the diner I let fix my breakfast those mornings I

can't face a frying pan, I watched a brown Chrysler pull out of the little parking area behind me in the rearview mirror. Three turns later it was still with me. I made a few more turns to make sure and then nicked the red light crossing John R. The Chrysler tried the same thing but had to brake when a Roadway van trundled through the intersection laying down horn.

I was still thinking about it when I squeezed into the visitors' lot outside Police Headquarters. My next alimony payment wasn't due for a month and I hadn't anything to do with the Sicilian boys' betterment league all year.

Sergeant Grandy had a worried-looking black woman in a ratty squirrel coat in the customer's chair and was clunking out a missing persons report with two fingers on a typewriter that came over with Father Marquette. I asked him if Lieutenant Winkle was in today.

"What for?" He mouthed each letter as he typed.

"Corcoran, same as yesterday."

"Go ahead and talk to him. I had a full head of hair before people started climbing over it."

I followed his thumb to where a slim black man in striped shirtsleeves and a plain brown tie was filling a china mug at the coffee maker. He wore a modest Afro and gray-tinted glasses. I gave him a card.

"I've been hired by Charlotte Corcoran to look for her ex-husband and their boy Tommy," I said. "The sergeant wasn't much help."

"Told you to walk off a dock, right?" His eyes might have twinkled over the top of the mug, but you can never be sure about cops' eyes.

"Words to that effect."

"Grandy's gone as high as he's going in my detail," he said. "No diplomacy. You have some identification besides a card?"

I showed him the chintzy pastel-colored ID the state hands out. He reached into a pocket and flipped forty cents into a tray full of coins next to the coffee maker. "Let's go into the cave."

We entered an office made of linoleum and amber pebbled glass, closing the door. He set down his mug, tugged at his trousers to protect the crease, and sat on the only clear corner of his desk. Then he pulled over his telephone and dialed a number.

"Hello, Miss Arnold? This is Lieutenant Winkle in General Service. . . . Millie, right. Is Mrs. Corcoran in? Thank you." Pause. "Mrs. Corcoran? No, I'm sorry, there's nothing new. Reason I called, I've got a private investigator here named Walker says he's working for you. . . . Okay, thanks. Just wanted to confirm it."

He hung up and looked at me. "Sorry. Department policy."

"I'm unoffendable," I said. "How many telephone numbers you keep in your head at a given time?"

"Last month I forgot my mother's birthday." He drowned his quiet smile in coffee. "We have nothing in the Corcoran case."

"Nothing as in nothing, or nothing you can do anything with?"

"Nothing as in zip. We run on coffee and nicotine here. When we get a box full of scraps we can hand over to the feds we don't waste time trying to assemble them ourselves. The FBI computer drew a blank on Corcoran."

"Not unusual if he doesn't have priors."

"It gets better. Because of the exodus from Michigan to Texas over the past couple of years a lot of local firms have been dealing with finance companies out there, so when it landed back in our lap we fed Great Western Loans and Credit into the department machine. Still nothing on Corcoran, because only the officers are on file. But the printout said the corporation invests heavily in government projects. As investments counselor, Frank Corcoran should have shown up on that FBI report. He'd have had to have been screened one time or another."

"Some kind of cover-up?"

"You tell me. The word's lost a lot of its impact in recent years."

I opened a fresh pack of Winstons. "So why keep Mrs. Corcoran in the dark?"

"Don't worry, it's not rubbing off on us," he said. "We're just holding her at arm's length till we get some answers back from channels. These things take time. Computer time, which is measured in Christmases."

"So why tell me?"

He smiled the quiet smile. "When Sergeant Grandy gave me your card I did some asking around the building. If you were a bulldog you'd have what the novelists call 'acquisitive teeth.' Quickest way to get rid of you guys is to throw you some truth."

"I appreciate it, Lieutenant." I rose and offered him my hand. He didn't give it back as hastily as some cops have. "Oh, what would you know about a brown Chrysler that was shadowing me a little while ago?"

"It wasn't one of mine," he said. "I'm lucky to get a blue-and-white when I want to go in with the band."

I grasped the doorknob. "Thanks again. I guess you're feeling better."

"Than what? Oh, yesterday. I called in sick to watch my kid pitch. He walked six batters in a row."

I grinned and left. That's the thing I hate most about cops. Find one that stands for everything you don't like about them and then you draw one that's human.

6

The job stank, all right. It stank indoors and it stank on the street and it stank in the car all the way to my building. I had the window closed this trip; the air was damp and the sky was throwing fingers whether to rain or snow. Michigan. But it wouldn't have smelled any better with the window down.

The pictures came out good, anyway. It must be nice to be in a business where if they don't you can trace the problem to a bad filter or dirt in the chemicals, something definite and impersonal that you can ditch and replace with something better. I left the fat photographer developing nude shots for a customer on Adult Row on Woodward and went upstairs.

I lock the waiting room overnight. I was about to use the key when the door swung inward and a young black party in faded overalls and a Pistons warm-up jacket grinned at me. He had a mouth built for grinning, wide as a Buick with door-to-door teeth and a thin moustache squared off like a bracket to make it seem even wider. "You're late, trooper," he said. "Let's you come in and we'll get started."

"Thanks, I'll come back," I said, and back-pedaled into something hard. The wall was closer this morning. A hand curled inside the back of my collar and jerked my suitcoat down to my elbows, straining the button and pinning my arms behind me.

Teeth drew a finger smelling of marijuana down my cheek. Then he balled his fist and rapped the side of my chin hard enough to make my own teeth snap together.

"Let's you come in, trooper. Unless you'd rather wake up smiling at yourself from your bedside table every morning."

I kicked him in the crotch.

He said, "Hee!" and hugged himself. Meanwhile I threw myself forward, popping the button and stripping out of my coat. My left arm was still tangled in the sleeve lining when I pivoted on my left foot and swung my right fist into a face eight inches higher than mine. I felt the jar clear to my shoulder. I was still gripping the keys in that hand.

The guy I hit let go of the coat to drag the back of a hand the size of a platter under his nose and looked at the blood. Then he took hold of my shirt collar from the front to steady me and cocked his other fist, taking aim.

"Easy, Del. We ain't supposed to bust him." Teeth's voice was a croak.

Del lowered his fist but kept his grip on my collar. He was almost seven feet tall, very black, and had artificially straightened hair combed into a high pompadour and sprayed hard as a brick. In place of a jacket he wore a full-length overcoat that barely reached his hips, over a sweatshirt that left his navel and flat hairy belly exposed.

Behind me Teeth said, "Del don't like to talk. He's got him a cleft palate. It don't get in his way at all. Now you want to come in, talk?"

I used what air Del had left me to agree. He let go and we went inside. In front of the door to my private office Teeth relieved me of my keys, unlocked it, and stood aside while his partner shoved me on through. Teeth glanced at the lock at his way in.

"Dead bolt, yeah. Looks new. You need one on the other door too."

He circled the room as he spoke and stopped in front of me. I was ready and got my hip out just as he let fly. I staggered sideways. Del caught me.

"That's no way to treat a client, trooper," Teeth said. "It gets around, pretty soon you ain't got no business."

"Client?" I shook off the giant's hand. My leg tingled.

Teeth reached into the slash pocket of his Pistons jacket and brought out a roll of crisp bills, riffling them under my nose. "Hundreds, trooper. Fifty of them in this little bunch. Go on, heft it. Ain't no heavier'n a roll of quarters, but, my oh my, how many more miles she draws."

He held it out while I got my coat right side in. Finally his arm got tired and he let it drop. I said, "You came in hard for paying customers. What do I have to forget?"

"We want someone to forget something we go rent a politician," he said. "Twenty-five hundred of this pays to look for somebody. The other twenty-five comes when the somebody gets found."

"Somebody being?" Knowing the answer.

"Same guy you're after now. Frank Corcoran."

"That standard for someone who's already looking for him for a lot less?"

"There's a little more to it," he said.

"Thought there might be."

"You find him, you tell us first. Ahead of his wife."

"Then?"

"Then you don't tell her."

"I guess I don't ask why."

His grin creaked. "You're smart, trooper. Too smart for poor."

"I'll need a number," I said.

"We call you." He held up the bills. "We talking?"

"Let's drink over it." I pushed past him around the desk and tugged at the handle on the deep drawer. Teeth's other hand moved and five inches of pointed steel flicked out of his fist. "Just a Scotch bottle," I said.

He leaned over the corner to see down into the drawer. I grabbed a handful of his hair and bounced his forehead off the desk. The switchblade went flying. Del, standing in front of the desk, made a growling sound in his chest and lurched forward. I yanked open the top drawer and fired my Smith & Wesson .38 without taking it out. The bullet smashed through the front panel and buried itself in the wall next to the door. It didn't come within a foot of hitting the big man. But he stopped. I raised the gun and backed to the window.

"A name," I said. "Whose money?"

Teeth rubbed his forehead, where a purple bruise was spreading under the brown. He stooped to pick up the currency from the floor and stood riffling it against his palm. His smile was a shadow of a ghost of what it had been. "No names today, trooper. I'm fresh out of names."

I said, "It works this way. You tell me the name. I don't shoot you."

"You don't shoot. Desks and walls, maybe. Not people. It's

why you're broke and it's why I get to walk around with somebody else's five long ones on account of it's what I drop on gas for my three Cadillacs."

"What about a Chrysler?"

"I pay my dentist in Chryslers," he said. "So long, trooper. Maybe I see you. Maybe you don't see me first. Oh." He got my keys out of his slash pocket and flipped them onto the desk. "We're splitting, Del."

Del looked around, spotted my framed original *Casablanca* poster hanging on the wall over the bullethole, and swung his fist. Glass sprayed. Then he turned around and crunched out behind his partner, speckling my carpet with blood from his lacerated fingers.

The telephone rang while I was cleaning the revolver. When I got my claws unhooked from the ceiling I lifted the receiver. It was Lieutenant Winkle. He wanted to see me at Headquarters.

"Something?" I asked.

"Everything," he said. "Don't stop for cigarettes on the way."

I reloaded, hunted up my holster, and clipped the works to my belt. No one came to investigate the shot. The neighborhood had fallen that far.

On Beaubien I left the gun in the car to clear the metal detectors inside. Heading there I walked past a brown Chrysler parked in the visitors' lot. There was no one inside and the doors were locked.

7

The lieutenant let me into his office, where two men in dark suits were seated in mismatched chairs. One had a head full of crisp gray hair and black-rimmed glasses astride a nose that had been broken sometime in the distant past. The other was younger and looked like Jack Kennedy but for a close-trimmed black beard. They stank federal.

"Eric Stendahl and Robert LeJohn." Winkle introduced them in the same order. "They're with the Justice Department."

"We met," I said. "Sort of."

Stendahl nodded. He might have smiled. "I thought you'd made us. I should have let Bob drive; he's harder to shake behind a wheel. But even an old eagle likes to test his wings now and then." The smile died. "We're here to ask you to stop looking for Frank Corcoran."

I lit a Winston. "If I say no?"

"Then we'll tell you. We have influence with the state police, who issued your license."

"I'll get a hearing. They'll have to tell me why."

"That won't be necessary," he said. "Corcoran was the inside man in an elaborate scheme to bilk Great Western Loans and Credit out of six hundred thousand dollars in loans to a nonexistent oil venture in Mexico. He was apprehended and agreed to turn state's evidence against his accomplices in return for a new identity and relocation for his protection. You're familiar with the alias program, I believe."

"I ran into it once." I looked at Winkle. "You knew?"

"Not until they came in here this morning after you left," he said. "They've had Mrs. Corcoran under surveillance. That's how they got on to you. It also explains why Washington turned its back on this one."

I added some ash to the fine mulch on the linoleum floor. "Not too bright, relocating him in an area where his ex-wife's cousin lives."

Stendahl said, "We didn't know about that, but it certainly would have clinched our other objections at the time. He spent his childhood here and had a fixation about the place. The people behind the swindle travel in wide circles; we couldn't chance his being spotted. Bob here was escorting Corcoran to the East Coast. He disappeared during the plane change at Metro Airport. We're still looking for him."

"It's a big club," I said. "We ought to have a secret handshake. What about Corcoran's son?"

LeJohn spoke up. "That's how he lost me. The boy was along. He had to go to the bathroom and he didn't want anyone but his father in with him. I went into the bookstore for a magazine. When I got back to the men's room it was empty."

"The old bathroom trick. Tell me, did Corcoran ever happen to mention that the boy was in his mother's custody and that you were acting as accomplices in his abduction?"

"He seemed happy enough," said LeJohn, glaring. "Excited about the trip."

His partner laid manicured fingers on his arm, calming him. To me: "It was a condition of Corcoran's testimony that the boy go with him to his new life. Legally, our compliance is indefensible. Morally — well, his evidence is expected to put some important felons behind bars."

"Yeah." I tipped some smoke out my nostrils. "I guess you got too busy to clue in Mrs. Corcoran."

"That was an oversight. We'll correct it while we're here."

"What did you mean when you said it was a big club?" LeJohn pressed me. "Who else is looking for Corcoran?"

I replayed the scene in my office. Lieutenant Winkle grunted. "Monroe Boyd and Little Delbert Riddle," he said. "I had one or both of them in here half a dozen times when I was with C.I.D. Extortion, suspicion of murder. Nothing stuck. So they're jobbing themselves out now. I'll put out a pickup on them if you want to press charges."

"They'd be out the door before you finished the paperwork. I'll just tack the price of a new old desk and a picture frame on to the expense sheet. The bullethole's good for business."

"How'd they know you were working for Mrs. Corcoran?" Stendahl asked.

"The same way you did, maybe. Only they were better at it."

He stood. "We'll need whatever you've got on them in your files, Lieutenant. Walker, you're out of it."

"Can I report to Mrs. Corcoran?"

"Yes. Yes, please do. It will save us some time. You've been very cooperative."

He extended his hand. I went on crushing out my cigarette in the ashtray on Winkle's desk until he got tired and lowered it. Then I left.

8

Millicent Arnold owned a condominium off Twelve Mile Road, within sight of the glass-and-steel skyscrapers of the Southfield Civic Center sticking up above the predominantly horizontal suburb like new teeth in an old mouth. A slim brunette with a pageboy haircut answered the bell wearing a pink angora sweater over black harem pants and gold sandals with high heels on her bare feet. Charlotte Corcoran might have looked like her before she had lost too much weight.

"Amos Walker? Yes, you are. My God, you look like a private eye. Come in."

I kept my mouth zipped at that one and walked past her into a living room paved with orange shag and furnished in green plush and glass. It should have looked like hell. I decided it was Millie Arnold standing in it that made it work. She hung my hat on an ornamental peg near the door.

"Charlotte's putting herself together. She was asleep when you called."

"She seems to sleep a lot."

"Her doctor in Austin prescribed a mild sedative. It's almost the only thing that's gotten her through this past month. You said you had some news." She indicated the sofa.

I took it. It was like sitting on a sponge. "The story hangs some lefts and rights," I said.

She sat next to me, trapping her hands between her knees. She wasn't wearing a ring. "My cousin and I are close," she said. "More like sisters. You can speak freely."

"I didn't mean that, although it was coming. I just don't want to have to tell it twice. I didn't like it when I heard it."

"That bad, huh?"

I said nothing. She tucked her feet under her and propped an elbow on the back of the sofa and her cheek in her hand. "I'm curious about something. I recommended Reliance to Charlotte. She came back with you."

"The case came down my street. Krell said she was referred to him by one of his cash customers."

She nodded. "Kester Clothiers on Lahser. I'm a buyer. I typed Charlotte's letter of reference on their stationery. The chain retains Reliance for security, employee theft and like that."

"I guess the hours are good."

"I'm off this week. We're between seasons." She paused. "You know, you're sort of attractive."

I was looking at her again when Charlotte Corcoran came in. She had on a maroon robe over a blue nightgown, rich material that bagged on her and made her wrists and ankles look even bonier than they were. Backless slippers. When she saw me her step quickened. "You found them? Is Tommy all right?"

I took a deep breath and sat her down in a green plush chair with tassels on the arms and told it.

"Wow," said Millie after a long silence.

I was watching her cousin. She remained motionless for a moment, then fumbled cigarettes and a book of matches out of her robe pocket. She tried to strike a match, said "Damn!" and threw the book on the floor. I picked it up and struck one and held the flame for her. She drew in a lungful and blew a plume at the ceiling. "The bastard," she said. "No wonder he never had time for me. He was too busy making himself rich."

"You didn't know about his testifying?" I asked.

"He came through with his child support on time. That's all I heard from him. It explains why he never came by for his weekends with Tommy." She looked at me. "Is my son in danger?"

"He is if he's with his father. Boyd and Riddle didn't look like lovers of children. But the feds are on it."

"This is the same federal government that endowed a study to find out why convicts want to escape prison?"

"Someone caught it on a bad day," I said.

"How much to go on with the investigation, Mr. Walker?"

"Nothing, Mrs. Corcoran. I just wanted to hear you say it."

She smiled then, a little.

"What progress have you made?" asked Millie.

"I'm chasing a lead now. If it gets any slimmer it won't be a lead at all. But it beats reading bumps." I got the package of prints out of my coat pocket, separated the original of Corcoran and Tommy from the others, and gave it back to Mrs. Corcoran. "I've got twenty-five more now, and at least that many places to show them. When I run out I'll try something else."

She looked at the picture. Seeing only one person in it. Then she put it in her robe pocket. "I think you're a good man, Mr. Walker."

Millie Arnold saw me to the door. "She's right, you know," she said, when I had it open. "You are good."

Attractive, too.

9

There was a gymnasium right around the corner on Greenfield. No one I talked to there recognized either of the faces in the picture, but I left it with the manager for seed along with my card and tried the next place on my list. I had them grouped by area with Southfield at the top. I hit two places in Birmingham, one in Clawson, then swung west and worked my way home in a loop through Farmington and Livonia. A jock in Redford Township with muscles on his T-shirt thought Corcoran looked familiar but couldn't finger him.

"There's fifty bucks in it for you when you do," I said. He flexed his trapezius and said he'd work on it.

I'd missed lunch, so I stopped in Detroit for an early supper, hit a few more places downtown, and went back to the office to read my mail and call my service for messages. I had none and the mail was all bills and junk. I locked up and went home. That night I dreamed I was Johnny Appleseed, but instead of trees every seed I threw sprang up grinning Monroe Boyds and hulking Delbert Riddles.

10

My fat photographer neighbor greeted me in the foyer of my building the next morning. He was chewing on what looked like the same Marlboro remnant and he hadn't been standing any closer to his razor than usual. "Some noise yesterday," he said. "Starting a range up there or what?"

"No, I shot a shutterbug for asking too many questions." I passed him on the stairs, no small feat.

With my gun drawn, I entered my office, felt stupid when I found it unoccupied, then saw the shattered glass from the poster frame and felt a little better. I swept it up and called my service. I had a message.

"Walker?" asked a male voice at the number left for me. "Tunk Herman, remember?"

"The guy in Redford," I said.

"Yeah. That fifty still good?"

"What've you got?"

"I couldn't stop thinking about that dude in the picture, so I went through the records of members. Thought maybe his name would jump out at me if I heard it, you know? Well, it did. James Muldoon. He's a weekender. I don't see him usually because I don't work weekends except that one time. I got an address for him."

I drew a pencil out of the cup on my desk. It shook a little.

11

It was spring now and no argument. The air had a fresh damp smell and the sun felt warm on my back as I leaned on the open-air telephone booth, or maybe it was my disposition seeping through from inside. Charlotte Corcoran answered on the eighth ring. Her voice sounded foggy.

"Walker, Mrs. Corcoran," I said. "Come get your son."

"What did you say? I took a pill a little while ago. It sounded —"

"It wasn't the pill. I'm looking at him now. Blond and blue, about four feet —"

The questions came fast, tumbling all over one another, too tangled to pull apart. I held the receiver away from my ear and waited. Down the block, on the other side of Pembroke, a little boy in blue overalls with a bright yellow mop was bouncing a ball off the wall of a two-story white frame house that went back forever. While I was watching, the front door came open and a dark-haired man beckoned him inside. Corcoran's physique was less impressive in street clothes.

"Tommy's fine," I said, when his mother wound down. "Meet me here." I gave her the address. "Put Millie on and I'll give her directions."

"Millie's out shopping. I don't have a car."

"Take a cab."

"Cab?"

"Forget it. You've got too much of that stuff in your pipes to come out alone. I'll pick you up in twenty minutes."

It was all of that. The road crews were at work and everyone who had a car and no job was out enjoying the season. I left the engine running in front of the brisk complex and bounced up the wrought-iron steps to where Millie's door stood open. I rapped and went inside. Charlotte Corcoran was sitting on the sofa in the robe and nightgown.

"That's out of style for the street this year," I said. "Get into something motherly."

"Plenty of time for that."

I felt my face get tired at the sound of the voice behind me. I turned around slowly. Millie Arnold was standing on the blind side of the door in a white summer dress with a red belt around her trim waist and a brown .32 Colt automatic in her right hand pointing at me.

"You don't look surprised." She nudged the door shut with the toe of a red pump.

"It was there," I said, raising my hands. "It just needed a kick. I had to wonder how Boyd and Riddle got on to me so fast. They couldn't have been following Mrs. Corcoran without Stendahl and LeJohn knowing. Someone had to tell them."

"It goes back farther than that. I made two calls to Texas after spotting Frank at the mall. The first was to his old partners. I can't tell you how much they appreciated it. If I did I'd be in trouble with the IRS. Then I called Charlotte. Throw the gun down on the rug, Mr. Walker. It made an ugly dent in my sofa when you were here yesterday."

I unholstered the .38 slowly. It hit the shag halfway between us with a thump. "Then, when Mrs. Corcoran arrived, you talked her into hiring the biggest investigative firm you knew. You figured to let them do the work of finding Corcoran. It probably meant a discount on Boyd and Riddle's fee."

"It also guaranteed me a bonus when Frank got dead," she

said. "Krell giving the case to you threw me, but it worked out just fine. When I got back from shopping and Charlotte gave me the good news I just couldn't wait to call our mutual friends and share it."

"My cousin," said Mrs. Corcoran.

Millie showed her teeth. Very white and a little sharp. "You married a hundred thou-a-year executive. I'd have settled for that. But if it wasn't enough for him, why should what I make be enough for me? I met his little playmates that time I visited you in Austin. I remembered them when it counted."

"What happens to us?" I asked.

"You'll both stay here with me until that phone rings. It'll be Boyd giving me thumbs up. I'll have to lock you in the bathroom when I leave, but you'll find a way out soon enough. You can have the condo, Charlotte. It isn't paid for."

"The boy had nothing to do with Corcoran's scam," I said. "You're putting him in front of the guns too."

"Rich kid. What do I owe him?"

"They won't hurt Tommy." Mrs. Corcoran got up.

"Sit down." The gun jerked.

But she was moving. I threw my arm in front of her. She knocked it aside and charged. Millie squeezed the trigger. It clicked. Her cousin was all over her then, kicking and shrieking and clawing at her eyes. It was interesting to see. Millie was healthier, but she was standing between a mother and her child. When the gun came up to clap the side of Mrs. Corcoran's head I tipped the odds, reversing ends on the Smith & Wesson I'd scooped up from the rug and tapping Millie behind the ear. Her knees gave then and she trickled through her cousin's grasp and puddled on the floor.

I reached down and pulled back her eyelids. "She's good for an hour," I said. "Call nine-one-one. Give them the address on Pembroke."

While she was doing that, breathing heavily, I picked up the automatic and ran back the action. Millie had forgotten to rack a cartridge into the chamber.

12

Approaching Pembroke we heard shots.

I jammed my heel down on the accelerator and we rounded the corner doing fifty. Charlotte Corcoran, still in her robe, gripped the door handle to stay out of my lap. Her profile was sharp against the window, thrust forward like a mother hawk's.

There was no sign of the police. As we entered Corcoran/ Muldoon's block, something flashed in an open upstairs window, followed closely by a hard flat bang. A much louder shot answered it from the front yard. There, a huge black figure in an overcoat too short for him crouched behind a lilac bush beside the driveway. His .44 magnum was as long as my thigh but looked like a kid's water pistol in his great fist.

"Hang on!" I spun the wheel hard and floored the pedal.

The Olds's engine roared and we bumped over the curb, diagonaling across the lawn. Del Riddle straightened at the noise and turned, bringing the magnum around with him. I saw his mouth open wide and then his body filled the windshield and I felt the impact. We bucked up over the porch stoop and suddenly the world was a deafening place of tearing wood and exploding glass. The car stopped then, although my foot was still pasted to the floor with the accelerator pedal underneath and the engine whining. The rear wheels spun shrilly. I cut the ignition. A piece of glass fell somewhere with a clank.

I looked at my passenger. She was slumped down in the seat with her knees against the dash. "All right?"

"I think so." She lowered her knees.

"Stay here."

The door didn't want to open. I shoved hard and it squawked against the buckled fender. I climbed out behind the Smith & Wesson in my right hand. I was in a living room with broken glass on the carpet and pieces of shredded siding slung over the chairs and sofa. Riddle lay spread-eagled on his face across the car's hood and windshield, groaning. His legs dangled like broken straws in front of the smashed grille.

"Lose the piece, trooper."

My eyes were still adjusting to the dim light indoors. I focused on Monroe Boyd baring his teeth in front of a hallway running to the back of the house. He had one arm around Tommy Corcoran's chest under the arms, holding him kicking above the floor. His other hand had a switchblade in it with the point pressing the boy's jugular.

"Tommy!" Charlotte Corcoran had gotten out on the passenger's side. She took a step and stopped. Boyd bettered his grip.

"Mommy," said the boy.

"What about it, trooper? Seven or seventy, they all bleed the same."

I relaxed my hold on the gun.

A shot slammed the walls and a blue hole appeared under Boyd's left eye. He let go of Tommy and lay down. Twitched once.

I looked up at Frank Corcoran crouched at the top of the staircase to the second story. His arm was stretched out full length with a gun at the end of it, leaking smoke. He glanced at Tommy. "I told you to stay upstairs with me."

"I left my ball here." The boy pouted, then spotted Boyd's body. "Funny man."

Mrs. Corcoran flew forward and knelt to throw her arms around her son. Corcoran saw her for the first time, said "Charlotte?" and looked at me. The gun came around.

"Stop waving that thing," his ex-wife said, hugging Tommy. "He's with me."

Corcoran hesitated, then lowered the weapon. He surveyed the damage. "What do I tell the rental agent?"

I heard the sirens then.

Bloody July

1

THE HOUSE was a half-timbered Tudor job on Kendall, standing on four acres fenced in by a five-foot ornamental stone wall. It wasn't the only one in the area and looked as much like metropolitan Detroit as it tried to look like Elizabethan England. A bank of lilacs had been allowed to grow over the wall inside, obstructing the view of the house from the street, but from there inward the lawn was bare of foliage, after the fashion of feudal estates to deny cover to intruders.

I wasn't one. As instructed previously, I stopped in front of the iron gate and got out to open it and was on my way back to the car when something black hurtled at me snarling out of the shrubbery. I clambered inside and shut the door and rolled up the window just as the thing leaped, scrabbling its claws on the roof and clouding the glass with its moist breath.

"Hector!"

At the sound of the harsh voice, the beast dropped to all fours and went on clearing its throat and glaring yellow at me through the window while a small man with a white goatee walked out through the gate and snapped a leash onto its collar. He wore a gray sportcoat and no tie.

"It's all right, Walker," he said. "Hector behaves himself while I'm around. You are Amos Walker."

I cranked the window down far enough to tell him I was, keeping my hand on the handle and my eye on the dog. "You're Mr. Blum?"

"Yeah. Drive on up to the house. I'll meet you there."

The driveway looped past an attached garage and a small front porch with carriage lamps mounted next to the door. I parked in front of the porch and leaned on the fender smoking a cigarette while Leonard Blum led the dog around back and then came through the house and opened the door for me. The wave of conditioned air hit me like a spray of cold water. It was the last day of June and the second of the first big heat wave of summer.

"You like dogs, Walker?"

"The little moppy noisy kind and the big gentle ones that lick your face."

"I like Dobermans. You can count on them to turn on you someday. With friends you never know." He ushered me into a dim living room crowded with heavy furniture and hung with paintings of square-riggers under full sail and bearded mariners in slick sou'westers shouting into the bow-wash. A varnished oak ship's wheel as big around as a hula hoop was mounted over the fireplace.

"Nautical, I know," said Blum. "I was in shipping a long time back. Never got my feet wet, but I liked to pretend I was John Paul Jones. That wheel belonged to the *Henry Morgan*, fastest craft ever to sail the river. In my day, anyway."

"That doesn't sound like the name of an ore carrier."

"It wasn't."

I waited, but he didn't embroider. He was crowding 80 if it wasn't stuck to his heels already, with heavy black-rimmed glasses and a few white hairs combed diagonally across his scalp and white teeth that flashed too much in his beard to be his. There was a space there when we both seemed to realize we were being measured, and then he said:

"My lawyer gave me your name. Simon Weintraub. You flushed out an eyewitness to an accident last year that saved his client a bundle."

"I'm pretty good." I waited some more.

"How are you at tracing stolen property?"

"Depends on the property."

He produced a key from a steel case on his belt, hobbled over to a bare corner of the room, and inserted the key in a slot I hadn't noticed. The wood paneling opened in two sections, exposing a recessed rectangle lined in burgundy plush and tall enough for a man to stand in.

"Notice anything?" he asked.

"Looks like a hairdresser's casket."

"It's a gun cabinet. An empty gun cabinet. Three days ago there wasn't enough room to store another piece in it."

"Were you at home when it got empty?"

"My wife and I spent the weekend on Mackinac Island. I've got a place there. Whoever did it, it wasn't his first job. He cut the alarm wires and picked the locks to the front door and the cabinet slick as spit."

"What about Hector?"

"I put him in a kennel for the weekend."

"Are you sure someone didn't just have a key?"

"The only key to this cabinet is on my belt. It's never out of my sight."

"Who else lives here besides your wife?"

"No one. We don't have servants. Elizabeth's at her CPR class now. I've got a heart I wouldn't wish on an Arab," he added.

"What'd the police say?"

"I didn't call them."

I was starting to get the idea. "Have you got a list of the stolen guns?"

He drew two sheets folded lengthwise out of his inside breast pocket, holding it back when I reached for it. "When does client privilege start?"

"When I pick up the telephone and say hello."

He gave me the list. It was neatly typewritten, the firearms identified by make, caliber, patent date, and serial number.

Some handguns, four high-powered rifles, a few antiques, two shotguns. And a Thompson submachine gun. I asked him if he was a dealer.

"No, I'm in construction."

"Non-dealers are prohibited from owning full automatic weapons," I said. "I guess you know that."

"I wanted a lecture I'd have gone to the cops to start."

"Also a warrant for your arrest. Are any of these guns registered, Mr. Blum?"

"That's not a question you get to ask," he said.

I handed back the list. "So long, Mr. Blum. I've got some business up in Iroquois Heights, so I won't charge you for the visit."

"Wait, Walker."

I had my back to him when he said it. It was the way he said it that made me turn around. It didn't sound like the Leonard Blum I'd been talking to.

"Nothing in the collection is registered," he said. "The rifles and shotguns don't have to be, of course, and I just never got around to doing the paper on the handguns and the Thompson. I've never been fingerprinted."

"It's an experience no one should miss," I said.

"I'll take your word for it. Anyway, that's why I didn't holler cop. For a long time now I've lived for that collection. My wife lays down for anything with a zipper; she's almost fifty years younger than me and it's no more than I have any right to expect. But pleasant memories are tied up with some of those pieces. I've seen what happens to old friends when they lose all interest, Walker. They wind up in wheelchairs stinking of urine and calling their daughters Charlie. I'd splatter my brains before I'd let that happen to me. Only now I don't have anything to do it with."

I got out one of my cards, scribbled a number on the back, and gave it to him. "Call this guy in Belleville. His name's Ben Perkins. He's a P.I. who doubles in apartment maintenance, which as lines of work go aren't so very different from each other. He's a cowboy, but a good one, which is what this job screams for. But I can't guarantee he'll touch it."

"I don't know." He was looking at the number. "Weintraub recommended you as the original clam."

"This guy makes me look like a set of those wind-up dime store dentures." I said so long again and let myself out, feeling cleansed. And as broke as a motel room chair.

2

The Iroquois Heights business had to do with a wandering wife I never found. What I did find was a deputy city prosecutor living off the town madam and a broken head courtesy of a local beat officer's monkey stick. The assistant chief is an old acquaintance. A week after the Kendall visit I was nursing my headache and the office fan with pliers and a paperclip when Lieutenant John Alderdyce of Detroit Homicide walked in. His black face glistened and he was breathing like a rhinoceros from the three-story climb. But his shirt and Chinese silk sportcoat looked fresh. He saw what I was doing and said, "Why don't you pop for air conditioning?"

"Every time I get a fund started I get hungry." I laid down my tools and plugged in the fan. The blades turned, wrinkling the thick air. I lifted my eyebrows at John.

He drew a small white rectangle out of an inside pocket and laid it on my desk, lining up the edges with those of the blotter. It was one of my business cards. "These things turn up in the damnedest places," he said. " So do you."

"I'm paid to. The cards I raise as best I can and then send them out into the world. I can't answer for where they wind up."

He flipped it over with a finger. A telephone number was

written on the back in a scrawl I recognized. I sighed and sat back.

"What'd he do," I asked, "hang himself or stick his tongue in a light socket?"

He jumped on it with both feet. "What makes it suicide?"

"Blum's wife was cheating on him, he said, and he lost his only other interest to a B-and-E. He as much as told me he'd take the back way out if that gun collection didn't find its way home."

"Maybe you better throw me the rest of it," he said.

I did, starting with my introduction to Blum's dog Hector and finishing with my exit from the house on Kendall. Alderdyce listened with his head down, stroking an unlit cigarette. We were coming up on the fifth anniversary of his first attempt to quit them.

"So you walked away from it," he said when I was through. "I never knew you to turn your back on a job just because it got too illegal."

I said, "We'll pass over that on account of we're so close. I didn't like Blum. When he couldn't bully me he tried wheedling, and he caught me in the wrong mood. Was it suicide?"

"It plays that way. Wife came home from an overnight stay with one of her little bridge partners and found him shot through the heart with a thirty-eight automatic. The gun was in his right hand and the paraffin test came up positive. Powder burns, the works. No note, but you can't have music too."

"Thirty-eight auto. You mean one of those Navy Supers?"

"Colt Sporting Pistol, Model Nineteen-Oh-Two. It was discontinued in nineteen twenty-eight. A real museum piece. The same gun was on a list we found in a desk drawer."

"I know the list. He said everything on it had been stolen."

"He lied. We turned your card in a wastebasket this morning. We tried to reach you."

"I was up in the Heights getting a lesson in police work, Warner Brothers style. Check out the wife's alibi?"

He nodded, rolling the cold cigarette along his lower lip. "A pro bowler in Harper Woods. You'd like him. Muscles on his elbows and if his IQ tests out at half his handicap you can have my pension. Blum started getting cold around midnight and she was at Fred Flintstone's place from ten o'clock on. She married Blum four years ago, about the time he turned seventy-five and handed over the operation of his construction firm to his partners. We're still digging."

"He told me he used to be in shipping." Alderdyce shrugged. I said, "I guess you called Perkins."

"The number you wrote on the card. Blum didn't score any more points with him than he did with you. I'm glad we never met. I wouldn't want to know someone who wasn't good enough for two P.I.'s with cardboard in their shoes."

I lit a Winston, just to make him squirm. "What I most enjoy paying rent on this office for is to provide a forum for over-dressed fuzz to run down my profession. Self-snuffings don't usually make you this pleasant. Or is it the heat?"

"It's the heat," he said. "It's also this particular self-snuffing. Maybe I'm burning out. They say one good way of telling is when you find yourself wanting to stand the stiff on its feet and ask it a question."

"As for instance?"

"As for instance, 'Mr. Blum, would you please tell me why before you shot yourself you decided to shoot your dog?' "

I said nothing. After a little while he broke his cigarette in two and flipped the pieces at my wastebasket and went out.

3

I finished my smoke, then broke out my Polk-administration Underwood and cranked a sheet into it and waited for my report to the husband of the runaway wife to fall into order. When I got tired of that I tore out the blank sheet and crumpled it and bonged it into the basket. My head said it was time to go home.

"Mr. Walker?"

I was busy locking the door to my private office. When I turned I was looking at a slender brunette of about 30 standing in the waiting room with the hall door closing on its pneumatic tube behind her. She wore her hair short and combed almost over one eye and had on a tailored black jacket that ran out of material just below her elbows, on top of a ruffled white blouse and a tight skirt to match the jacket. Black purse and shoes. The weather was too hot for black, but she made it look cool.

I got my hat off the back of my head and said I was Walker.

She said, "I'm Andrea Blum. Leonard Blum is — was my husband."

I unlocked the door again and held it for her. Inside the brain room she glanced casually at the butterfly wallpaper and framed *Casablanca* poster and accepted the chair I held for her, the one whose legs were all the same length. I sat down behind the desk and said I was sorry about Mr. Blum.

She smiled slightly. "I won't pretend I'm destroyed. It's no secret our marriage was a joke. But you get used to having someone around, and then when he's not —" She spread her hands. "Leonard told me he tried to hire you to trace his stolen guns and that you turned him down."

"I'd have had to tell the police that a cache of unregistered firearms was loose," I said. "Three out of five people in this town carry guns. They'd like to keep the other two virgin."

"Don't explain. I was just as happy they were taken. Guns frighten me. Anyway, that's not why I'm here. The police think Leonard's death was self-inflicted."

"You don't."

She moved her head. The sunlight caught a reddish thread in her black hair. "The burglary infuriated him. After that other detective refused to take the case he was determined to find one that would. He was ready to do it himself if it came to that. Do people shoot themselves when they're angry, Mr. Walker?"

"Never having shot myself I can't say."

"And he wouldn't have killed Hector," she went on. "He loved that dog. Besides, where could he have gotten the gun? It was one of those missing."

"Could be the burglars overlooked it and he just didn't tell you. And it wouldn't be the first time a suicide took something he loved with him. Generally it's the wife. You're lucky, Mrs. Blum."

"That he cared less for me than he did for his dog? I deserve that, I guess. Marrying an old man for his money gets boring. All those other men were just a diversion. I loved Leonard in my way." She lined up her fingers primly on the purse in her lap. The nails were sharp and buffed to a high gloss, no polish. "He didn't kill himself. Whoever killed him shot the dog first when it came at him."

I offered her a cigarette from the deck. When she shook her head I lit one for myself and said, "I've got a question, but I don't want one of those nails in my eye."

"Insurance," she said. "A hundred thousand dollars, and I'm the sole beneficiary. It's worth more than twice the estate minus debts outstanding. And yes, if suicide is established as cause of death the policy is void. But that's only part of why I'm here, though I admit it's the biggest part. At the very least I owe it to Leonard to find out who murdered him."

"Who do you suspect?"

"I can't think of anyone. We seldom had visitors. He outlived most of his friends and the only contact he had with his business partners was over the telephone. He was in semiretirement."

She gave me the name of the firm and the partners' names. I wrote them down. "What did your husband do before he went into construction?" I asked.

"He would never tell me. Whenever I asked he'd say it

didn't matter, those were dead days. I gather it had something to do with the river but he never struck me as the sailor type. May could tell you. His first wife. May Shinstone, her name is now. She lives in Birmingham."

I wrote that down too. "I'll look into it, Mrs. Blum. Until the cops stop thinking suicide, anyway. They frown on competition. Meanwhile I think you should find another place to stay."

"Why?"

"Because if Mr. Blum was murdered odds are it was by the same person who stole his guns, and that person sneezes at locks. If you get killed I won't have anyone to report to."

After a moment she nodded. "I have a place to stay."

I believed her.

4

When she had left, poorer by a check in the amount of my standard three-day retainer, I called Ben Perkins. We swapped insults and then I drew on a favor he owed me and got the number of a gun broker downtown, one who wasn't listed under Guns in the Yellow Pages. Breaking the connection I could almost smell one of the cork-tipped ropes Perkins smokes. When he lit one up in your presence you wouldn't have to see him pull it out of his boot to know where he keeps them.

Eleven rings in, a voice with a Mississippi twang came on and recited the number I had just dialed.

"I'm a P.I. named Walker," I said. "Ben Perkins gave me your number."

He got my number and said he'd call back. We hung up.

Three minutes later the telephone rang. It was Mississippi. "Okay, Perk says you're cool. What?"

"I need a line on some hot guns," I said.

"Nix, not over the squawker. What's the tag?"

"Fifty, if you've got what I want."

"Man, I keep a roll of fifties in the crapper. Case I run out of Charmin, you know? A hunnert up front. No refunds."

"Sixty-five. Fifty up front. Nothing if I don't come away happy."

"Sevenny-five and no guarantees. Phone's gettin' *heavy*, man."

I said okay. We compared meeting places, settling finally on a city parking lot on West Lafayette at six o'clock.

My next call was to Leonard Blum's construction firm, where a junior partner referred me to Ed Klagan at a building site on Third. Klagan's was one of the names Andrea Blum had given me. I asked for the number at the building site.

"There aren't any phones on the twenty-first floor, mister," the junior partner told me.

An M. Shinstone was listed in Birmingham. I tried the number and cradled the receiver after twenty rings. It was getting slippery. I got up, peeling my shirt away from my back, stood in front of the clanking fan for a minute, then hooked up my hat and jacket. The thermometer at the bank where I cashed Mrs. Blum's check read 87°, which was as cool as it had been all day.

5

It was hotter on Third Street. The naked girders straining up from the construction site were losing their vertical hold in the smog and twisting heat waves, and the security guard at the opening in the board fence had sweated through his light blue uniform shirt. I shouted my business over the clattering pneumatic hammers. At length he signaled to a broad party in a hardhat and necktie who was squinting at a blueprint in the hands of a glistening half-naked black man. The broad party came over, getting bigger as he approached until I was looking up at his Adam's apple and three chins folded over it. The guard left us.

"Mr. Klagan?"

"Yeah. You from the city?"

"The country, originally." I showed him my ID. "Andrea Blum hired me to look into her husband's death."

"I heard he croaked himself."

"That's what I'm being paid to find out. What was his interest in the construction firm?"

"Strictly financial. Pumped most of his profits back into the business and arranged an occasional loan when we were on the shorts, which wasn't often. He put together a good organization. Look, I got to get back up on the steel. The higher these guys go the slower they work. And the foreman's a drunk."

"Why don't you fire him?"

He uncovered tobacco-stained teeth in a sour grin. "Local two-two-six. Socialism's got us by the uppers, brother."

"One more question. Blum's life before he got into construction is starting to look like a mystery. I thought you could clear it up."

"Not me. My old man might. They started the firm together."

"Where can I find him?"

"Mount Elliott. But you better bring a shovel."

"I was afraid it'd be something like that," I said.

"All I know is Blum came up to the old man in January of 'thirty-four with a roll of greenbacks the size of a coconut and told him he looked too smart to die a foreman. He had the bucks, Pop had the know-how."

He showed me an acre of palm and moved off. I smoked a cigarette to soothe a throat made raw by yelling over the noise and watched him mount the hydraulic platform that would take him up to the unfinished twenty-first floor. Thinking.

6

The parking lot on West Lafayette was in the shadow of the *News* building; stepping into it from the heat of the street was like falling headfirst into a pond. I stood in the aisle, mopping the back of my neck with my soaked handkerchief and looking around. My watch read six on the nose.

A horn peeped. I looked in that direction. The only vehicle occupied was a ten-year-old Dodge club cab pickup parked next to the building with Michigan cancer eating through its rear fenders and a dull green finish worn down to brown primer in leprous patches. I went over there.

The window on the driver's side came down, leaking loud music and framing a narrow, heavy-lidded black face in the opening. "You a P.I. named Walker?"

I said I was. He reached across the interior and popped up the lock button on the passenger's side. The cab was paved with maroon plush inside and had an instrument-studded leather dash and speakers for a sound system that had cost at least as much as the book on the pickup, pouring out drums and electric guitars at brain-throbbing volume. He'd had the air conditioner on recently and it was ten degrees cooler inside.

My eardrums had been raped enough for one day. I shouted to him to turn down the roar. He twirled a knob and then it was just us and the engine ticking as it cooled.

My host was a loose tube of bones in a red tank top and blue running shorts. And alligator shoes on his bare feet. He caught me looking at them and said, "I got an allergy to everything but lizard. You carrying?"

When I hesitated he showed me the muzzle of a nickel-plated .357 magnum he had lying face down on his lap. I didn't think he was the *Ebony* type. I took the Smith & Wesson out of its belt holster slowly and handed it to him butt first. His lip curled.

"Police Special. Who you, Dick Tracy? I got what you want here." He laid my revolver on his side of the dash and snaked an arm over the back of the seat into the compartment behind. After some rummaging he came up with a chromed Colt Python as long as my forearm. "Man, you plug them with this mother, the lead goes through them, knocks down a light pole across the street."

"I've got no beef with Detroit Edison."

He dropped his baggy grin, put the big magnum back behind the seat and its little brother on the dash next to my .38, and held out his palm. I laid seventy-five dollars in it. He folded the bills and slid them under a clip on the sun visor. "You after hot iron."

"Just its history." I recited Blum's list so far as I remembered it. "They came up gone from a house on Kendall a little over a week ago," I added. "Unless someone's hugging the ground they should be on the market by now. Some of those pieces are pretty rare. You'd know them."

"Ain't come my way. I can let you have a forty-five auto Army, never issued. Two hunnert."

"How many notches?"

"Man, this a virgin piece. The barrel, anyway."

"The guns," I said. "You'd hear if they were available. It's a lot of iron to hit the street all at one time."

"When S 'n' W talks, people listen. Only I guess it missed me."

"Okay, hang your ears out. I've got another seventy-five says they'll show up soon." I gave him my card.

"Last week a fourteen-year-old kid give me that much for a Saturday night banger I don't want to be in the same *building* with when it goes off. Listen, I can put you behind a Thompson Model Nineteen Twenty-One for a thousand. The Gun That Won Chicago. Throw in a fifty-round drum."

I looked back at him with my hand on the door handle. I'd clean forgotten that item on Blum's list. "You've got a Thompson?"

His eyes hooded over. "Could be I know where one can be got."

I peeled three fifties off the roll in my pocket and held them up.

"I trade you a thousand-dollar piece for a bill and a half? Get out of my face, turkey white meat." He turned on the sound system. The pickup's frame buzzed.

"Ooh, jive," I said, turning it off. "You keep the gun. All I want is the seller's name. There's a murder involved."

He hesitated. I skinned off another fifty. He put his fingers on them. I held on.

"I call you, man," he said.

I tore the bills in two and gave him half. "You know the speech."

"Ain't no way to treat President Grant." But he clipped the torn bills with the rest and gave me back my gun, tipping out the cartridges first. There's no more trust in the world.

7

Shadows were lengthening downtown, cooling the pavement without actually lowering the temperature. I caught a sandwich and a cold beer at a counter and used the pay telephone to try the Birmingham number again. A husky female voice answered.

"May Shinstone?"

"Yes?"

I told her who I was and what I was after. There was a short silence before she said, "Leonard's dead?"

I made a face at the snarl of penciled numbers on the wall next to the telephone. "I'm sorry, Mrs. Shinstone. I got so used to it I forgot everyone didn't know."

"Don't apologize. It was just a surprise. It's been two years since I've seen Leonard, and almost that long since I've thought about him. I don't know how I can help you."

"Just now I'm sweeping up whatever's lying around. I'll sort it out later. I need some stuff on his life before January nineteen thirty-four."

"That isn't a story for the telephone, Mr. Walker."

There was something in her tone. I played around with it for a second, then poked it into a drawer. "If you have a few minutes this evening I'd like to come talk to you about it," I said.

"How big is your car trunk?"

"Would you say that again, Mrs. Shinstone? We have a bad connection."

"I'm giving up the house here and moving to an apartment in Royal Oak. I have one or two things left to move. If your trunk's big enough I can dismiss the cab I have waiting." She gave me her address.

I said, "I'll put the spare tire in the back seat."

I paused with my hand on the receiver, then unhooked it again and used another quarter to call my service. Lieutenant Alderdyce had tried to reach me and wanted me to call him back. I dialed his extension at Headquarters.

"I spoke to Mrs. Blum a little while ago," he said. "You're fired."

"Funny, you don't sound like her."

"She'll tell you the same thing. Blum's death is starting not to look like suicide and that means you can go back to your bench and leave the field to the first string."

"How much not like suicide is it starting to look?"

"Just for the hell of it we ran Blum's prints. We got a positive."

"He told me he'd never been printed."

"He must've forgot," Alderdyce said. "We didn't mess with the FBI. They destroy their records once a subject turns seventy. We got a match in a box of stuff on its way to the incinerator because it was too old to bother feeding into the computer. There is no Leonard Blum. But Leo Goldblum got to know these halls during Prohibition, whenever the old rackets squad found it prudent to round up the Purple Gang and ask questions."

"Blum was a Purple?"

"Nice kids, those. When they weren't gunning each other down and commuting to Chicago to pull off the St. Valentine's Day Massacre for Capone they found time to ship bootleg hooch across the river from Canada. That was Goldblum's specialty. He was arrested twice for transporting liquor from the Ecorse docks and drew a year's probation in 'twenty-nine on a Sullivan rap. Had a revolver in his pocket."

"Explains why he never registered his guns," I said. Licenses aren't issued to convicted felons. "That was a long time ago, John."

"Yeah, well, there's something else. Ever hear of Bloody July?"

"Sounds like the name of a punk rock group. No, wasn't that when they killed Jerry Buckley?"

"The golden boy of radio. Changed his stand on the mayor's recall on July twenty-second, nineteen thirty, and a few hours later three Purples left him in a pool of blood in the lobby of the Hotel LaSalle. And during the first two weeks of the month the gang got frisky and put holes in ten of their Mob playmates. It was a good month not to be a cop."

"All this history is leading someplace, I guess."

"Yeah. We got a lot of eager young uniforms here. One of them spent a couple of hours after his shift was over pawing through dusty records in the basement and matched the bullet that killed Blum with the ballistics report on the shooting of one Emmanuel Eckleberg, DOA at St. Mary's Hospital July sixth, nineteen thirty."

"Yesterday was July sixth," I said. "You're telling me someone waited all these years to avenge Manny Whatsizname on the anniversary of his death with the same gun that was used to kill him?"

"Eckleberg. You want someone to tell you that, call Hollywood. I just read you what we've got. You're walking, right?"

"Give me some time to square away a couple of things for my report."

He might have said "Uh-oh." I can't be sure because I was hanging up. It was getting to be a hell of a case, all right.

8

The address I wanted in Birmingham belonged to a small crackerbox with blue aluminum siding and a rosebush that had outgrown its bed under the picture window. My watch read seven-thirty and the sky showed no signs of darkening. You get a lot more for your money by hiring a private investigator in the summertime.

My knock was answered by a tall slim woman in sweats with blond streaks in her gray hair drawn up under a knotted handkerchief. She had taken the time to put on lipstick and rub rouge into her cheeks, but she really didn't need it. She had to be in her early seventies but looked twenty years younger. Her eyes were flat blue.

She smiled. "You look like you were expecting granny glasses and a ball of yarn."

"I was sort of looking forward to it," I said, taking off my hat. "No one seems to knit any more except football players."

"I never could get the knack. Come in."

The place looked bigger inside, mainly because there was hardly any furniture in it and the walls and floor were bare. She led me to a heavy oak table with the round top removed and leaning against the pedestal base. "Will it fit?" she asked.

"Search me. I flunked physics." I put my hat back on and got to work.

It was awkward, but the top eventually slid onto the ledge where the spare belonged and the pedestal fit diagonally into the well. She carried out a carton of books and slid it onto the back seat. "Take Telegraph down to Twelve Mile," she said, getting in on the passenger's side in front.

On the road I asked if Mr. Shinstone was waiting for her in Royal Oak.

"He died in 'seventy-eight. I would have sold the place then, but my sister got sick and I took her in. She passed away six weeks ago."

I said I was sorry. She shrugged. "You were married to Leonard Blum when he was Leo Goldblum?" I asked.

She looked at me, then untied her handkerchief and shook her hair loose. She kept it short. "You've been doing your homework. Have you got a cigarette?"

I got out two, lit them from the dash lighter, and gave her one. She blew smoke into the slipstream outside her window. "I started seeing him when I was in high school," she said. "He was twenty and very dashing. They all were; handsome boys in sharp suits and shiny new automobiles. We thought they were Robin Hoods. Never mind that people got killed, it was all for a good cause. The right to get hung over. The world was different then."

"Just the suits and automobiles," I put in. "Prohibition was repealed in December nineteen thirty-three. In January nineteen thirty-four, Goldblum shortened his name and invested his bootlegging profits in construction."

"He and Ed Klagan, Sr., had a previous understanding. I don't know how many buildings downtown are still being held up by people Leo didn't get on with. Mind you, I only suspected these things at the time."

"Was Manny Eckleberg one of them?"

"Who was he?"

I told her as much as I knew. We were stopped at a light and I was watching her. She was studying the horizontal suburban scenery. "I think I remember it. It was during that terrible July. Leo and some others were questioned by the police. Somebody was convicted for it. Abe Somebody; my sister dated him once or twice. Leo and I were married soon after and I remember hoping it wouldn't mean a postponement."

"Why was he killed?"

"A territorial dispute, I suppose. It was a long time ago."

"Did you divorce Blum because of his past?"

"I could say that and sound noble. But I just got tired of being married to him. That was twenty years ago and he was already turning into an old crab. From what I saw of him during the times I ran into him since I'd say he never changed. Turn right here."

She had three rooms and a bath in the back half of a house on Farnum. I carried the table inside and set both pieces down in the middle of a room full of cartons and furniture. She added the box of books to the pile. "Thank you, Mr. Walker. You're a nice man."

"Mrs. Shinstone," I said, "can you tell me why Blum might have been killed by the same gun that killed Manny Eckleberg?"

"Heavens, no. You said he was killed by a gun from his collection, didn't you?" I nodded. "Well, I guess that tells us something about the original murder then, doesn't it? Not that it matters."

She let me use her telephone to call my service. I had a message. I asked the girl from whom.

"He wouldn't leave his name, just his number." She gave it to me. I recognized it.

This time it rang fourteen times before the voice came on. "What've you got for me, Mississippi?" I asked.

"They's a parking lot on Livernois at Fort," he said. "Good view of the river."

"No more parking lots. Let's make it my building in half an hour."

I broke the connection, thanked Mrs. Shinstone, and got out of her new living room.

9

The sky was purpling finally when I stepped into the foyer of my office building. A breeze had come up to peel away the smog and humidity. I mounted the stairs, stopping when something stiff prodded my lower back.

"Turn around, turkey white meat."

The something stiff was withdrawn and I obeyed. The lanky gun broker had stepped out from behind the propped-open fire door and was standing at the base of the stairs in his summer running outfit and alligator shoes. His right hand was wrapped around the butt of a lean automatic.

"Bang, you dead." He flashed a grin and reversed the gun, extending the checked grip. "Go on, see how she feels. Luger. Ninety bucks."

I said, "That's not a Luger. It's a P-thirty-eight."

"Okay, eighty-five. 'Cause you discerning."

"Keep the gun. I'm getting my fill of them." I produced my half of the two hundred I'd torn earlier, holding it back when he reached for it.

He moved a shoulder and clipped the pistol under his tank top. "He goes by Shoe. I don't know his right name. White dude, big nose. When he turns sideways everything disappears but that beak. Tried to sell me the tommy gun and some other stuff on your list. Told him I had to scratch up cash. He says call him here." He handed me a fold of paper from the pocket of his shorts. "Belongs to a roach hatchery at Wilson and Webb."

"This better be the square." I gave him the abbreviated currency.

"Hey, I deal hot merchandise. I got to be honest."

10

They had just missed the hotel putting through the John Lodge and that was too bad. It was eight stories of charred brick held together with scaffolding and pigeon-splatter. An electric sign ran up the front reading   O   L PON   C. After five minutes I gave up wondering what it was trying to say and went inside. A kid in an Afro and army BVD undershirt looked up from the copy of *Bronze Thrills* he was reading behind the desk as I approached. I said, "I'm looking for a white guy named Shoe. Skinny guy with a big nose. He lives here."

"If his name ain't Smith or Jones it ain't in the register." He laid a dirty hand on the desk, palm up.

I rang the bell on the desk with his head and repeated what I'd said.

"Twenty-three," he groaned, rubbing his forehead. "Second floor, end of the hall."

It had been an elegant hall, with thick carpeting and wainscoting to absorb noise, but the floorboards whimpered now under the shiny fabric and the plaster bulged over the dull oak. I rapped on 23. The door opened four inches and I was looking at a smoky brown eye and half a nose the size of my fist.

"I'm the new house man," I said. "We got a complaint you've been playing your TV too loud."

"Ain't got a TV." He had a voice like a pencil sharpener.

"Your radio, then."

The door started to close. I leaned a shoulder against it. When it sprang open I had to change my footing to keep my face off the floor. He was holding a short-barreled revolver at belly level.

A day like that brought a whole new meaning to the phrase Detroit iron.

"You're the dick, let's see your ID."

I held it up.

"Okay. I'm checking out tonight anyway." The door closed.

I waited until the lock snapped, then walked back downstairs, making plenty of noise. I could afford to. I'd had a good look at Shoe and at an airline ticket folder lying on the lamp table next to the door.

I passed the reader in the lobby without comment and got into my crate parked across the street in front of a mailbox. While I was watching the entrance and smoking a cigarette, a car rolled up behind mine and a fat woman in a green dress levered herself out to mail a letter and scowl at me through the windshield. I smiled back.

The streetlights had just sprung on when Shoe came out lugging two big suitcases and turned into the parking lot next door. Five minutes later a blue Plymouth with a smashed fender pulled out of the lot and the light fluttered on a big-nosed profile. I gave him a block before following.

We took the Lodge down to Grand River and turned right onto Selden. After three blocks the Plymouth slid into a vacant space just as a station wagon was leaving it. I cruised on past and stopped at the next intersection, adjusting my rearview mirror to watch Shoe angle across the street on foot, using both hands on the bigger of the two suitcases. He had to set it down to open a lighted glass door stenciled ZOLOTOW SECURITIES, then brace the door with a foot while he backed in towing his burden.

I found a space around the corner and walked back. Two doors down I leaned against the closed entrance to an insurance office, fired a Winston, and chased mosquitoes with the glowing tip while Shoe was busy striking a deal with the pawnbroker.

He was plenty scared, all right.

It was waiting time, the kind you measure in ashes. I was on my third smoke when a blue-and-white cut into the curb in front of Zolotow's and a uniform with a droopy gunfighter's moustache got out from behind the wheel.

The glass door opened just as the cop had both feet on the pavement. He drew his side arm and threw both hands across the roof of the prowl car. "Freeze! Police!"

Empty-handed, Shoe backpedaled. The cop yelled freeze again, but he was already back inside. The door drifted shut. A second blue-and-white wheeled into the block, and then I heard sirens.

A minute crawled past. I counted four guns trained on the door. Blue and red flashers washed the street in pulsing light. Then the door flew open again and Shoe was on the threshold cradling a Chicago typewriter.

Someone hollered, "Drop it!"

Thompsons pull to the left and up. The muzzle splattered fire, its bullets sparking off the first prowl car's roof and pounding dust out of the granite wall across the street and shattering windows higher up, tok-tok-tok-tok-tok.

The return shots came so close together they made one long roar. Shoe slammed back against the door and slid into a sitting position spraddle-legged in the entrance, the submachine gun in his lap.

As the uniforms came forward, guns out, an unmarked unit fishtailed into the street. Lieutenant Alderdyce was out the passenger's side while it was still rocking on its springs. He glanced down at the body on the sidewalk, then looked up and spotted me in the crowd of officers. "What the hell are you doing here?"

"Mainly, abusing my lungs," I said. "How about you?"

"Pawnbroker matched the guns this clown was selling to the hot sheet. He made an excuse and called us from the back."

I said, "He was running scared. He had a plane ticket and he checked out of the hotel where he was living. He was after a getaway stake."

"The murder hit the radio tonight. When his suicide scam went bust he rabbited."

The plainclothesman who had come with Alderdyce leaned out the open door of the pawnshop. Shoe was acting as a doorstop now. "He had all the handguns in the suitcase except one or two, John."

"Hey, this guy's still alive."

Everyone looked at the uniform down on one knee beside Shoe. The wounded man's chest rose and fell feebly beneath his bloody shirt. Alderdyce leaned forward.

"It's over," he said. "No sense lying your way deeper into hell. Why'd you kill Blum?"

Shoe looked up at him. His eyes were growing soft. After a moment his lips moved. On that street with the windows going up on both sides and police radios squawking it got very quiet.

11

It was even quieter on Farnum in Royal Oak, where night lay warm on the lawns and sidewalks and I towed a little space of silence through ratcheting crickets on my way to the back door of the duplex. The lights were off inside. I rang the bell and had time to smoke a cigarette between the time they came on and when May Shinstone looked at me through the window. A moment later she opened the door. Her hair was tousled and she had on a blue robe over a lighter blue nightgown that covered her feet. Without make-up she looked older, but still nowhere near her true age.

"Isn't it a little late for visiting, Mr. Walker?"

"It's going to be a busy night," I said. "The cops will be here as soon as they find out you've left the place in Birmingham and get a change of address."

"I don't know what you're talking about, but come in. When I was young we believed the night air was bad for you."

She closed the door behind me. The living room looked like a living room now. The cartons were gone and the books were in place on the shelves. I said, "You've been busy."

"Yes. Isn't it awful? I'm one of those compulsive people who can't go to sleep when there's a mess to be cleaned up."

"You can't have gotten much sleep lately, then. Leaving Shoe with all those guns made a big mess."

"Shoe? I don't —"

"The cops shot him at the place where he tried to lay them off. When he found out he was mixed up in murder he panicked. He made a dying statement in front of seven witnesses."

She was going to brazen it out. She stood with her back to the door and her hands in the pockets of her robe and a marble look on her face. Then it crumbled. I watched her grow old.

"I let him keep most of what he stole," she said. "It was his payment for agreeing to burgle Leo's house. All I wanted was the Colt automatic, the thirty-eight he used to kill Manny Eckleberg. Shoe — his name was Henry Schumacher — was my gardener in Birmingham. I hired him knowing of his prison record for breaking and entering. I didn't dream I'd ever have use for his talents in that area."

"You had him steal the entire collection to keep Blum from suspecting what you had in mind. Then on the anniversary of Eckleberg's murder you went back and killed him with the same gun. Pure poetry."

"I went there to kill him, yes. He let me in and when I pointed the gun he laughed at me and tried to take it away. We struggled. It went off. I don't expect you to believe that."

"It doesn't matter what I believe because it stinks first-degree any way you smell it," I said. "So you stuck his finger in the trigger afterwards and fired the gun through the window or something to satisfy the paraffin test and make it look like suicide. Why'd you kill the dog?"

"After letting me in, Leo set it loose in the grounds. It wouldn't let me out the door. I guess he'd trained it to trap intruders until he called it off. So I went back and got the gun and shot it. That hurt me more than killing Leo, can you imagine that? A poor dumb beast."

"What was Manny Eckleberg to you?"

"Nothing. I never knew him. He was just a small-time bootlegger from St. Louis who thought he could play with the Purple Gang."

I said nothing. Waiting. After a moment she crossed in front of me, opened a drawer in a bureau that was holding up a china lamp, and handed me a bundle of yellowed envelopes bound with a faded brown ribbon.

"Those are letters my sister received from Abe Steinmetz when he was serving time in Jackson prison for Eckleberg's murder," she said. "In them he explains how Leo Goldblum paid him to confess to the murder. He promised him he wouldn't serve more than two years and that there would be lots more waiting when he got out. Only he never got out. He was stabbed to death in a mess room brawl six months before his parole.

"I was the one who was dating Abe, Mr. Walker; not my sister. I was seeing him at the same time I was seeing Leo. He swore her to secrecy in the letters, believing I wouldn't understand until he could explain things in person. The money would start our marriage off right, he said. But instead of waiting I married Leo."

She wet her lips. I lit a Winston and gave it to her. She inhaled deeply, her fingers fidgeting and dropping ash on the carpet. "My sister kept the secret all these years. It wasn't until she died and I opened her safety deposit box and read the letters —" She broke off and mashed out the cigarette in a copper ashtray atop the bureau. "Do I have time to get dressed and put on lipstick before the police arrive? They never even gave Leo time to grab a necktie whenever they took him in for questioning."

I told her to take as much time as she needed. At the bedroom door she paused. "I don't regret it, you know. Maybe I wouldn't have been happy married to Abe. But when I think of all those wasted years — well, I don't regret it." She went through the door.

Waiting, I pocketed the letters, shook the last cigarette out of my pack, and struck a match. I stared at the flame until it burned down to my fingers.

He had all the handguns in the suitcase except one or two.

I dropped the match and vaulted to the bedroom door. Moving too damn slowly. I had my hand on the knob when I heard the shot.

12

The temperatures soared later in the month, and with them the crime statistics. The weathermen called it the hottest July on record. The newspapers had another name for it, but it had already been used.